# *ANIMA*

GEORGE

Stag
Retold by Catherine Skliarova

GET IT ON Google Play

Download on the App Store

Sesli kütüphanemize yukarıdaki karekodu okutarak veya Google Play / App Store üzerinden MK Publications yazarak ulaşabilirsiniz.

MK PUBLICATIONS

**MK** PUBLICATIONS

(Murat Kurt Kitapçılık ve Kırtasiye)
MK Plaza, Ferhatpaşa Mah. 22. Sk. No.50
34888 Ataşehir / İstanbul
Tel : (9) 0216 469 50 15
Web : www.mkpublications.com.tr
e-mail : info@mkpublications.com.tr

ISBN: 978-625-7289-19-1
Sertifika No: 47283
SECOND EDITION – OCTOBER 2021



Author: George Orwell
Retold by: Catherine Skliarova
Proof Read by: Zoe Ferris
Series Editor: Murat Kurt
Cover Design: Ibrahim Mısır
Picture Researcher: Burak Kurt
Cover Photograph: iStockphoto

Printed in Istanbul

Pasifik Ofset
Cihangir Mah. Güvercin Cad. No:3/1 Baha İş Merkezi
A Blok Kat:2 34310 Haramidere / İSTANBUL
Tel: (9) 0212 412 17 77
www.pasifikofset.com.tr
Sertifika: 44451

## *Contents*

## Chapter 1

Mr Jones, of the Manor Farm, had locked the hen-houses for the night. With the ring of light from his lantern dancing from side to side, he walked across the yard, took off his boots at the back door, and made his way up to the bed, where Mrs Jones was already sleeping. As soon as the light in the bedroom went out there was a moving and noise all through the farm buildings. The thing was that old Major, a white boar, had had a strange dream on the previous night and wished to tell it to the other animals. They agreed to meet in the big barn as soon as Mr Jones was safely out of the way. Old Major (so he was always called) was so highly respected on the farm that everyone was quite ready to lose an hour's sleep to hear what he had to say. At one end of the big barn, on a sort of raised platform, Major lay on his bed of straw, under a lantern which hung from a beam. He was twelve years old. He was a majestic-looking pig with a wise appearance. Before long the other animals began to arrive and make themselves comfortable after their different fashions. First came the three dogs, Bluebell, Jessie, and Pincher, and then the pigs, who settled down in the straw immediately in front of the platform. The hens got into the window-sills, the pigeons fluttered up to the rafters, the sheep and cows lay down behind the pigs and began to chew the cud. The two horses, Boxer and Clover, came in together, walking very slowly and setting down their hairy hoofs with great care. Clover was a big middle-aged mare. Boxer was a big strong horse. He had a white stripe down his nose. He was not very intelligent, but he was respected for his kind character and hard work. After the horses came Muriel, the white goat, and Benjamin, the donkey. Benjamin was the oldest animal on the farm. He seldom talked, and when he did, it was usually to make some small remark. He never laughed. If asked why, he would say that he saw nothing to laugh at. Nevertheless, without admitting it, he was devoted to Boxer; the two of them usually spent their Sundays together in the small paddock beyond the orchard. Just then a brood of ducklings, which had lost their mother, came into the barn, moving from side to side to find some place where they would not be comfortable. Clover made a sort of wall round them with her great foreleg, and the ducklings nestled inside it and soon fell asleep. At the last moment Mollie, a stupid, pretty white mare came slowly in, chewing at a lump of sugar. She took a place near the front, hoping to draw attention to the red ribbons in her mane. Last of all came the cat, who looked round, as usual, for the warmest place, and finally squeezed herself in between Boxer and Clover; there she purred contentedly throughout Major's speech without listening to a word of what he was saying. All the animals were now present except Moses, the tame raven, who slept on a perch behind the back door. When Major saw that they had all made themselves comfortable and were waiting attentively, he cleared his throat and began:

"Friends, you have heard already about the strange dream that I had last night. But I will tell you about my dream later. I have something else to say first. I do not think, friends, that I will be with you for many months longer, and before I die, I feel it is my duty to share with you my wisdom. I have had a long life. I have had much time for thought as I lay alone in my stall. I think I may say that I understand the nature of life on this earth as well as any animal now living. It is about this that I wish to speak to you. Now, friends, what is the nature of this life of ours? Let us be frank. Our lives are miserable, laborious, and short. We are born, we are given just so much food as will keep the breath in our bodies. When our usefulness has come to an end we are killed with cruelty. No animal in England knows the meaning of happiness or leisure after he is a year old. No animal in England is free. The life of an animal is misery and slavery. That is the truth.

Is the land of England poor? No, friends, a thousand times no! The soil of England is fertile and its climate is good. The land of England can afford food in abundance to a great number of animals. Our farm can support a dozen horses, twenty cows, and hundreds of sheep! Why then do we live in this miserable condition? Because the result of our work is taken from us by human beings. There is the answer to all our problems. It is a single word – Man. Man is the only real enemy we have. If we remove Man from the farm, and the hunger and hard work will finish forever! Man is the only creature that consumes without producing. He does not give milk, he does not lay eggs, he is too weak to pull the plough, he cannot run fast enough to catch rabbits. Yet he is lord of all the animals. He makes them work, he gives minimum food to them, and the rest he keeps for himself.There is not one of us that has more than his bare skin. You cows that I see before me, how many thousands of gallons of milk have you given during this last year? Every drop of it has gone down the throats of our enemies. And you hens, how many eggs have you laid in this last year, and how many of those eggs ever turned into chickens? The rest have all gone to market to bring in money for Jones and his men. And you, Clover, where are those four foals that you bore? Each was sold at a year old. You will never see one of them again. In return for your four foals and all your work in the fields, what have you ever had except your small rations and a stall?

As for me, I am twelve years old. I have had over four hundred children. Such is the natural life of a pig. But no animal escapes the cruel knife in the end. You, young porkers who are sitting in front of me, every one of you will be killed within a year. To that horror we all must come: cows, pigs, hens, sheep, everyone. Even the horses and the dogs have no better fate. You, Boxer, Jones will sell you to the knacker. As for the dogs, when they grow old, Jones ties a brick round their necks and drowns them in the nearest pond. Is it not clear, friends, that all the evils of our life have come from the tyranny of human beings? Only get rid of Man, and the produce of our work would be our own. We can become rich and free. What then must we do? We must work night and day to overthrow of the human race! That is my message to you: Rebellion! I do not know when that Rebellion will come. It might be in a week or a hundred years. But I know, as surely as I see this straw beneath my feet, that sooner or later justice will come. Pass on this message to those who come after you. Pass on my message to future generations! And remember, friends, your resolution must never fail. Do not be afraid! Do not hesitate! Never listen when they tell you that Man and the animals have a common interest, that the prosperity of the one is the prosperity of the others. It is all lies. Man is interested only in himself. And among us, animals, let there be perfect unity and perfect friendship in the struggle. All men are enemies. All animals are friends."

At this moment there was a tremendous roar. While Major was speaking four large rats had crept out of their holes and were listening to him. The dogs suddenly saw them, and it was only thanks to a quick movement for their holes that the rats saved their lives. Major raised his trotter for silence.

"Friends," he said, "I have something more to say. The wild creatures, such as rats and rabbits, are they our friends or our enemies?Let us answer this question. I propose this question to the meeting: Are rats friends?"

The animals answered at once. The majority came to the agreement that rats were friends. There were only four opponents, the three dogs and the cat. Major continued:

"I repeat, remember always your duty of fight against Man. Whatever goes on two legs is an enemy. Whatever goes upon four legs, or has wings, is a friend. And remember also that in fighting against Man, we must not resemble him. Even when you have conquered him, do not resemble him. No animal must ever live in a house, or sleep in a bed, or wear clothes, or drink alcohol, or smoke tobacco, or touch money, or engage in trade. All the habits of Man are evil. And, above all, no animal must ever hurt his own kind. Weak or strong, clever or simple, we are all brothers. No animal must ever kill any other animal. All animals are equal. And now, friends, I will tell you about my dream that I had last night. In my dream, there was no Man on earth. This dream reminded me of one song. Many years ago, when I was a little pig, my mother used to sing an old song. Last night, that song came back to me in my dream.I will sing you that song now, friends. It is called, *the Beast of England*."

Old Major cleared his throat and began to sing. The words ran:

*Beast of England, beasts of Ireland,*
*Beasts of every land and kind,*
*Listen to my joyful news,*
*About the golden future time.*
*Sooner or later, the day is coming,*
*Cruel Man will be conquered,*
*And the fruitful fields of England*
*Will belong to beasts alone.*
*Rings will vanish from our noses,*
*And the harness from our back,*
*Cruel whips no more will crack.*
*Wheat and barley, oat and hay,*
*Will be ours upon that day.*
*Bright will shine the fields of England,*
*On the day that sets us free.*
*For that day we all must work,*
*Though we die before it begins,*
*Cows and horses, geese and turkeys,*
*All must work for freedom's sake.*

The singing of this song made animals very excited. Almost before Major reached the end, they began singing it for themselves. Even the stupidest of them picked up the tune and a few of the words, and as for the clever ones, such as the pigs and dogs, they learned the entire song by heart within a few minutes. And then, after a few tries, the whole farm was singing *the Beasts of England.* They were so happy with the song that they sang it many times. Unfortunately, a roar in the barn awoke Mr Jones. He jumped out of bed, making sure that there was a fox in the yard. He took the gun which always stood in a corner of his bedroom, and fired it six times into the darkness. The bullets buried themselves in the wall of the barn and the meeting came to the end at once. Everyone ran to his own sleeping-place. The birds jumped on to their perches and the animals lay down in the straw. The whole farm was asleep in a moment.

## Chapter 2

Three nights later old Major died peacefully in his sleep. His body was buried at the foot of the orchard. This was early in March. During the next three months, there was much secret activity. Major's speech had given to the animals on the farm a completely new view on life. They did not know when the Rebellion predicted by Major would happen. They had no reason for thinking that it would happen within their own life. But they knew that it was their duty to prepare for it. The pigs taught and organized the others because they were the cleverest of animals. Among the pigs, there were two young boars named Snowball and Napoleon, whom Mr Jones was breeding up for sale. Napoleon was a large boar who did not like talking. Snowball was smaller than Napoleon, better in speech and more inventive. All the other male pigs on the farm were porkers. The best known among them was a small fat pig named Squealer, with very round cheeks, twinkling eyes, slow movements, and a loud voice. He was a brilliant talker. These three had developed old Major's teachings into a complete system of thought, to which they gave the name of Animalism. Several nights a week, when Mr Jones was asleep, they held secret meetings in the barn and explained the principles of Animalism to the others. In the beginning, they met with such stupidity and apathy. Some of the animals talked of the duty of loyalty to Mr Jones, whom they called "Master," or made remarks such as "Mr Jones feeds us." Others asked such questions as "Why should we care what happens after we are dead?" or "If this Rebellion will happen anyway, what difference does it make whether we work for it or not?" The pigs had great difficulty in making them see that this was against the principles of Animalism. The stupidest questions of all were asked by Mollie, the white mare. The first question she asked Snowball was: "Will there still be sugar after the Rebellion?"

"No," said Snowball. "We cannot make sugar on this farm. Besides, you do not need sugar. You will have all the oats and hay you want."

"And will I still be able to wear ribbons in my mane?" asked Mollie.

"Mollie," said Snowball, "those ribbons that you love so much are the badge of slavery. Can you not understand that freedom is worth more than ribbons?"

Mollie agreed, but she did not sound very convinced.

The pigs had an even harder struggle against Moses's lies. Moses was the tame raven. Moses, who was Mr Jones's special pet, was a spy. He was also a clever talker. He always talked about a mysterious country called Sugarcandy Mountain, to which all animals went when they died. It was situated somewhere up in the sky, a little distance beyond the clouds, Moses said. In Sugarcandy Mountain, it was Sunday seven days a week, clover was in season all the year round, and lump sugar grew on the hedges. The animals hated Moses because he told tales and did no work. But some of them believed in Sugarcandy Mountain, and the pigs had to argue very hard to persuade them that there was no such place.

The pigs' most faithful students and helpers were the two horses, Boxer and Clover. These two accepted the pigs as their teachers. They absorbed everything that they were told and passed it on to the other animals by simple words. They were always present at the secret meetings in the barn, and led the singing of *the Beasts of England*, with which the meetings always ended.

The Rebellion happened much earlier and more easily than anyone had expected. In past years, Mr Jones had become very unlucky after losing money in a lawsuit. For many days he would sit in his chair in the kitchen, reading the newspapers, drinking, and sometimes feeding Moses on crusts of bread. His men were lazy. The fields were full of weeds, the buildings were dirty, the hedges were neglected, and the animals were hungry. June came and the hay was almost ready for cutting. One day, Mr Jones went into Willingdon and got so drunk that he did not come back till midday on Sunday. The men had gone to bed without bothering to feed the animals. When Mr Jones got back, he immediately went to sleep. The animals were still hungry. At last, they could stand it no longer. One of the cows broke in the door of the store with her horn and all the animals began to eat from the bins. It was just then that Mr Jones woke up. The next moment he and his four men were in the store-shed with whips in their hands, lashing out in all directions. This was more than the hungry animals could bear. They ran towards their tormentors. They kicked Jones and his men from all sides. The situation was quite out of their control. They had never seen animals behave like this before. They were frightened. After only a moment or two, Jones and his men gave up trying to defend themselves and ran away.

A minute later all five of them were on the main road, with the animals pursuing them in triumph.

Mrs Jones looked out of the bedroom window. She saw what was happening. She put a few things into a bag and ran out of the farm by another way. Moses jumped off his perch and flew after her, croaking loudly. Meanwhile, the animals chased Jones and his men out on to the road and closed the gate behind them. And so, almost before they knew what was happening, the Rebellion happened successfully. Jones was expelled, and the Manor Farm belonged to them. For the first few minutes, the animals could hardly believe in their good fortune. Their first act was to run around the farm, as though to make sure that no human being was hiding anywhere. Then they ran back to the farm buildings to destroy the last traces of Jones's reign. After that, they came into the harness-room at the end of the stables. They opened the harness-room. The reins, the whips, the nose-rings, the dog-chains, the cruel knives were all flung down the well. Soon the animals had destroyed everything that reminded them of Mr Jones. All the animals cried with joy. Napoleon then led them back to the store-shed and gave a double ration of corn to everybody, with two biscuits for each dog. Then they sang *the Beasts of England* seven times. After that, they settled down for the night and slept as they had never slept before.

They woke in the morning as usual, and suddenly remembered the glorious thing that had happened. They all ran out into the pasture together. A little way down the pasture, there was a hill that gave a view of most of the farm. The animals ran to the top of it and looked around them in the clear morning light. Yes, it was theirs – everything that they could see belonged to them! They rolled round and round, they jumped into the air in great excitement. They rolled in the dew, they ate sweet summer grass, they kicked up the black earth and sniffed its scent. Then they made a tour of inspection of the whole farm. They inspected the ploughland, the hayfield, the orchard, and the pool. It was as though they had never seen these things before. Even now they could hardly believe that it was all their own. Then they went back to the farm buildings and waited in silence outside the door of the farmhouse. That belonged to them too, but they were frightened to go inside. After a moment, however, Snowball and Napoleon opened the door with their shoulders and the animals came in carefully. They walked slowly. They walked from room to room, afraid to speak loudly and looking with fear at the unbelievable luxury, at the beds with their feather mattresses, the looking-glasses, the horsehair sofa, the carpet, and the clock over the drawing-room mantelpiece. They were just coming down the stairs when Mollie was discovered to be missing.Going back, the others found her in the best bedroom. She took a piece of blue ribbon from Mrs Jones's dressing-table and was holding it against her shoulder and admiring herself in the glass. When she saw her companions, she quickly ran out of the house. The animals went outside. They touched nothing in the house. They decided that the farmhouse should be kept as a museum. They agreed that no animal must ever live there. The animals had their breakfast, and then Snowball and Napoleon called them together again.

"Comrades," said Snowball, "it is half-past six and we have a long day before us. Today we begin the hay harvest. But another thing must be done at first."

The pigs now said that during the past three months they had taught themselves to read and write from an old spelling book which had belonged to Mr Jones's children and which had been thrown on the rubbish heap. Napoleon then brought pots of black and white paint. Snowball (who was best at writing) took a brush between his trotters and painted out ANIMAL FARM on the gate. This was to be the name of the farm now. After that, they went back to the farm buildings, where Snowball and Napoleon sent for a ladder. When the animals brought the ladder, Snowball and Napoleon set the ladder against the wall of the big barn. They explained that during the past three months the pigs had reduced the principles of Animalism to Seven Commandments. They wanted to paint these Seven Commandments on the wall. With some difficulty (because it is not easy for a pig to balance himself on a ladder) Snowball climbed up and began to paint, with Squealer below him holding the paint-pot. Snowball painted the Commandments on the wall in large black letters. They were the following:

***The Seven Commandments***

*1) Whatever goes on two legs is an enemy.*

*2) Whatever goes on four legs, or has wings, is a friend.*

*3) No animal will wear clothes.*

*4) No animal will drink alcohol.*

*5) No animal will sleep in a bed.*

*6) No animal will kill any other animal.*

*7) All animals are equal.*

The spelling was correct. Snowball read it aloud to the other animals. All the animals nodded in complete agreement, and the cleverer ones at once began to learn the Commandments by heart.

"Now, friends," cried Snowball, "to the hayfield! Let us get in the harvest more quickly than Jones and his men could do!"

But at this moment the three cows cried loudly. Nobody had milked them for twenty-four hours, and their udders were almost bursting. After a little thought, the pigs sent for buckets and milked the cows quite well. Soon there were five buckets full of milk at which many animals looked with great interest. They did not know what to do with that milk.

"What is going to happen to all that milk?" said someone.

"Jones mixed some of it in our mash," said one of the hens.

"Never mind the milk, friends! We will do something with it. The hay is waiting. Snowball will lead you to the hayfield. I will follow you in a few minutes."

So the animals went to the hayfield to begin the harvest. When they came back in the evening, they noticed that the milk had disappeared.

## Chapter 3

How they worked and sweated to get the hay in! But their efforts were not in vain, because the harvest was a bigger success than they had hoped. Sometimes the work was hard. The tools had been designed for human beings and not for animals. Besides, almost every tool needed standing on his hind legs. But the pigs were so clever that they could find a solution for every difficulty. As for the horses, they knew every part of the field and understood the business of ploughing far better than Jones and his men had ever done. The pigs did not actually work, but directed and supervised the others. With their superior knowledge, it was natural that they should take the leadership. Boxer and Clover would harness themselves to the horse-rake and move steadily round and round the field with a pig walking behind and calling out "Move forward, friend!" or "Move back, friend!" And every animal worked at turning the hay and gathering it. Even the ducks and hens worked all day in the sun, carrying tiny wisps of hay in their beaks. In the end, they finished the harvest in two days' less time than it had usually taken Jones and his men. Moreover, it was the biggest harvest that the farm had ever seen. The hens and ducks with their sharp eyes had gathered up the very last stalk. Nobody stole a thing.

All through that summer, the work of the farm went like clockwork. The animals were happy as they had never thought it possible to be. Every piece of food was very tasty, now that it was truly their food, produced by themselves and for themselves. There was more for everyone to eat. There was more leisure too. They met with many difficulties. For example, later in the year, they had to tread the corn out in the old style, since the farm possessed no threshing machine. But the pigs with their cleverness and Boxer with his muscles always pulled them through. Boxer was the admiration of everybody. He had been a hard worker even in Jones's time, but now he seemed more like three horses than one. There were days when the whole work of the farm seemed to rest on his strong shoulders. From morning to night, he was pushing and pulling, always at the place where the work was hardest. He woke up early in the morning before the regular day's work began. His answer to every problem was "I will work harder!" This phrase became his motto. But everyone worked according to his capacity. The hens and ducks, for example, saved five bushels of corn at the harvest by gathering up the stray grains. Nobody stole, nobody complained about his rations. Quarrelling and jealousy which had been usual in the old days had disappeared.

However, Mollie was not good at getting up in the mornings. She left work early on the ground, saying that there was a stone in her hoof. And the behaviour of the cat was somewhat strange. When there was work to be done the cat could never be found. She would disappear for hours and then come again at meal-times, or in the evening after work was over, as though nothing had happened. She always made excellent excuses and purred loudly. Only Benjamin, the donkey, seemed quite unchanged since the Rebellion. He did his work in the same slow way as he had done it in Jones's time. He never asked for extra work. About the Rebellion and its results he would express no opinion. One day, Boxer asked him whether he was happier now. He said only:

"Donkeys live a long time. None of you has ever seen a dead donkey."

On Sundays there was no work. Breakfast was an hour later than usual, and after breakfast there was a ceremony which was done every week. First came the hoisting of the flag. One day, Snowball had found in the harness-room an old green tablecloth of Mrs Jones's. He painted on it a hoof and a horn in white. He ran up the flagstaff in the farmhouse garden every Sunday morning. The flag was green. It represented the green fields of England, while the hoof and horn represented the future Republic of the Animals. After the hoisting of the flag, all the animals went into the big barn for a general meeting. Here they planned the work of the coming week. It was always the pigs who took decisions. The other animals understood how to vote, but could never think of any decisions. Snowball and Napoleon were the most active in the debates. But these two were never in agreement. The meeting always ended with the singing of *the Beasts of England*, and the afternoon was given up to rest.

The pigs had set aside the harness-room as a headquarters for themselves. Here, in the evenings, they studied blacksmithing, carpentering, and other necessary arts from books which they had brought out from the farmhouse. Snowball also was busy with organizing the other animals into what he called Animal Committees. He formed the Egg Production Committee for the hens, the Clean Tails League for the cows, the Whiter Wool Movement for the sheep, the Re-education for wild animals and many others, besides giving classes in reading and writing.The cat joined the Re-education Committee and was very active in it for some days. She was seen one day sitting on a roof and talking to some sparrows who were just out of her reach. She was telling them that the animals were now friends and that any sparrow who chose could come and touch her paw. But the sparrows kept their distance. The reading and writing classes were a great success. By the autumn almost every animal on the farm could read and write in some way. As for the pigs, they could already read and write perfectly. The dogs learned to read quite well, but were not interested in reading anything except the Seven Commandments. Muriel, the goat, could read somewhat better than the dogs. Benjamin could read as well as any pig. Clover learned the whole alphabet, but could not put words together. Boxer could not get beyond the letter D. He could write A, B, C, D, in the dust with his hoof, and then would stand staring at the letters with his ears back, trying to remember what came next and never succeeding. Finally, he decided that the first four letters were enough for him, and used to write them out once or twice every day to refresh his memory. Mollie refused to learn any but the six letters which spelt her name.None of the other animals on the farm could get further than the letter A. The stupider animals, such as the sheep, hens, and ducks could not learn the Seven Commandments by heart. After much thought, Snowball decided that the Seven Commandments could be reduced to a single commandment: "Four legs good, two legs bad." This, he said, was the main principle of Animalism. The birds at first protested, since it seemed to them that they also had two legs, but Snowball proved to them that this was not so.

“A bird’s wing, friends,” he said, “should be regarded as a leg.”

The birds accepted his explanation, and all the stupider animals began to learn the new commandment by heart. FOUR LEGS GOOD, TWO LEGS BAD, was written on the wall of the barn, above the Seven Commandments and in bigger letters.

Napoleon took no interest in Snowball’s committees. He said that the education of the young was more important than for those who were already grown up. It happened that Jessie gave birth to nine puppies. As soon as they began to eat food, Napoleon took them away from their mother, saying that he would make himself responsible for their education. He took them up into a loft which could only be reached by a ladder. There he kept them all the time. Soon the animals forgot about their existence. The mystery of where the milk went was soon cleared up. It was mixed every day into the pig’ mash. The early apples were now ripening. The animals decided to share the apples equally. However, one day, the pigs decided that the apples should belong to the pigs alone. All the pigs were in full agreement on this point, even Snowball and Napoleon. Squealer went into the barn to make the necessary explanations to the others.

“Friends! Many of you dislike milk and apples. But milk and apples are necessary to the health of a pig. We pigs are brainworkers. The whole management and organization of this farm depend on us. Day and night we think of your happiness.”

The animals were completely sure that they did not want Jones back. They had nothing to say. The importance of keeping the pigs in good health was clear to them. So the milk and the apples belonged the pigs alone.

## Chapter 4

By the late summer, the news of what had happened on Animal Farm spread across half the county. Every day Snowball and Napoleon sent out pigeons whose duties were to talk with the animals on neighbouring farms, tell them the story of the Rebellion, and teach them the song of *the Beasts of England.* Most of this time Mr Jones spent sitting in the pub of the Red Lion at Willingdon, complaining to anyone who would listen of the injustice he had suffered on Manor Farm. The other farmers sympathised in general, but they did not at first give him much help. Actually, each of them was secretly wondering whether he could not somehow turn Jones's misfortune to his advantage. One of them, the owner of Foxwood Farm, Mr Pilkington, was an easy-going gentleman farmer who spent most of his time in fishing or hunting according to the season. The other farm, which was called Pinchfield, was smaller in size. Its owner was a Mr Frederick. Mr Pilkington and Mr Frederick disliked each other so much that it was difficult for them to come to any agreement, even in defence of their interests. Nevertheless, they were both frightened by the rebellion on Animal Farm. They did not want their animals to learn too much about it. At first, they pretended to laugh at the idea of animals managing a farm for themselves. The whole thing would be over in a week or two, they said. They said that the animals on the Manor Farm were fighting among themselves and were also starving to death. When time passed and the animals had not starved to death, Frederick and Pilkington stopped spreading rumours about Animal Farm.

However, nobody believed in their stories. Rumours of a wonderful farm managed by animals continued to circulate through the countryside. Bulls turned wild, sheep broke down hedges and ate the clover, and cows kicked the pail over. Above all, the song and even the words *the Beasts of England* were known everywhere. It spread with astonishing speed. Human beings could not hold their anger when they heard this song. They could not understand how animals could sing such a ridiculous song. And yet the song was irrepressible. The blackbirds whistled it in the hedges and the pigeons sang it in the elms. And when the human beings listened to it, they secretly trembled, hearing in it a prophecy of their future doom.

In early October, a flight of pigeons came whirling through the air and stopped in the yard of Animal Farm in the wildest excitement. Jones and all his men, with half a dozen others from Foxwood and Pinchfield, were coming up to the farm. They were all carrying sticks, except Jones, who was walking ahead with a gun in his hands. They were going to attack the farm! The animals expected this long ago, and all preparations had been made. Snowball, who had studied an old book of Julius Caesar's campaigns, was a leader of the defensive operations. He gave his orders quickly, and in a couple of minutes, every animal was at his post. As human beings came closer to the farm buildings, Snowball launched his first attack. All the pigeons flew to and fro over the men's heads and muted on them from the air. While the men were dealing with this, the geese, who were hiding behind the hedge, rushed out and pecked angrily at the calves of their legs. However, Snowball planned to create only a little disorder. The men easily drove the geese off with their sticks. Snowball now launched his second line of attack. Muriel, Benjamin, and all the sheep, with Snowball at the head of them, ran forward and attacked the men from every side, while Benjamin turned around and attacked them with his small hoofs. But once again the men, with their sticks and their heavy boots, were too strong for them. Suddenly, Snowball cried loudly. His cry was the signal for retreat. All the animals turned and ran through the gateway into the yard. The men gave a cry of triumph. They saw, as they imagined, their enemies in flight, and they ran after them quickly. This was just what Snowball wanted. As soon as they were well inside the yard, the three horses, the three cows, and the rest of the pigs, suddenly cut them off. Snowball now gave the signal for the attack. He himself ran straight for Jones. Jones saw him coming, raised his gun and fired. A sheep dropped dead. Without waiting for an instant, Snowball attacked Jones. Jones fell and his gun flew out of his hands. But the most terrifying spectacle of all was Boxer, standing on his hind legs and striking out with his great hoofs. He attacked a man with his large hoofs. The man lay lifeless in the mud. At the sight, several men dropped their sticks and tried to run. Panic overtook them, and the next moment all the animals together were chasing them round and round the yard. There was not an animal on the farm that did attack the men after his own fashion. Even the cat suddenly jumped off a roof on a man's shoulders and sank her claws in his neck, at which he cried horribly. At a moment when the opening was clear, the men were glad enough to run out of the yard and make their way for the main road. And so after five minutes, they were running by the same way as they had come, with a flock of geese running after them and pecking at their calves all the way.

All the men were gone except one. Back in the yard Boxer was standing next to the senseless man who lay face down in the mud. Boxer was trying to turn him over. The man did not move.

"He is dead," said Boxer sadly. "I did not want to do that. I forgot that I was wearing iron shoes. I did not do this on purpose?"

"Don't be sentimental, my friend!" said Snowball. "War is war. You have done nothing wrong."

"I had no wish to take life, not even human life," said Boxer, and his eyes were full of tears.

"Where is Mollie?" asked somebody.

Mollie was missing. For a moment there was great alarm. The men could harm her in some way, or even carry her off with them. In the end, however, they found Mollie in her stall with her head buried among the hay. She ran away as soon as the gun went off. And when the others came back from looking for her, they found that the senseless man had already recovered and ran away.

The animals now gathered with the wildest excitement, each explaining his exploits in the battle at the top of his voice. A celebration of the victory was held immediately. The flag was run up and *the Beasts of England* was sung many times. Then they buried the sheep who had been killed in the battle. At the graveside Snowball made a little speech, talking about the need for all animals to be ready to die for Animal Farm if need be. The animals decided quickly to create a military decoration, "Animal Hero, First Class" which was given to

Snowball and Boxer. It was a brass medal (they were some old horse-brasses which had been found in the harness-room). There was also “Animal Hero, Second Class,” which was given immediately to the dead sheep. There was much discussion as to what the battle should be called. In the end, it was named the Battle of the Cowshed. They found Mr Jones’s gun in the mud. There were some bullets left in the cartridges. The animals decided to fire it twice a year – once on October the twelfth, the anniversary of the Battle of the Cowshed, and once on Midsummer Day, the anniversary of the Rebellion.

the farm with electrical power. This would light the stalls and warm them in the winter, and would also run an electric milking machine. The animals had never heard of anything of this windmill before (because the farm was an old-fashioned one and had only the most primitive machinery). They listened in surprise while Snowball showed them pictures of fantastic machines which would do their work for them while they rested in the fields or improved their minds with reading and writing.

Within a few weeks, Snowball's plans for the windmill were fully ready. The mechanical details came mostly from three books which had belonged to Mr Jones – "One Thousand Useful Things to Do About the House", and "Electricity for Beginners". Snowball used a shed for his study room. It had a smooth wooden floor, suitable for drawing on. He stayed there for hours at a time. Slowly his plans grew into complicated schemes, covering more than half the floor, which the other animals found strange but very impressive. All of them came to look at Snowball's drawings at least once a day. Even the hens and ducks came to look at his drawings. Only Napoleon did not come into Snowball's study room. He had declared himself against the windmill from the start. One day, however, he came secretly to examine the plans. He walked silently round the shed, looked closely at every detail of the plans, then suddenly he lifted his leg, scattered the plans, and walked out without saying a word.

The whole farm was divided on the subject of the windmill. Snowball did not deny that to build it would be a difficult business. They would have to carry heavy stones and build them up into walls. Snowball did not say how he planned to do that. But he said that it could all be done in a year. He also said that the animals would work three days a week. Napoleon argued that they must increase food production, and that if they wasted time on the windmill they would all starve to death. The animals formed themselves into two groups under the slogan, "Vote for Snowball and the three-day week" and "Vote for Napoleon and the full stomach." Benjamin was the only animal who did not side with either faction. Windmill or no windmill, he said, life would go on as usual. Apart from the disputes over the windmill, there was the question of the defence of the farm. The human beings had been defeated in the Battle of the Cowshed. However, they might attack Animal Farm once again. They had more reasons for doing so because the news of their defeat had spread across the countryside and made the animals on the neighbouring farms more popular than ever. As usual, Snowball and Napoleon were in disagreement. According to Napoleon, the animals must create some kind of weapons and train themselves in the use of them. According to Snowball, they must send out more and more pigeons and stir up rebellion among the animals on the other farms. The animals listened first to Napoleon, then to Snowball, and could not decide which was right. Actually, they always found themselves in agreement with the one who was speaking at the moment.

At last, the day came when Snowball's plans were completed. At the meeting on the following Sunday, the animals began to vote whether or not to begin to work on the windmill. When the animals gathered in the big barn, Snowball stood up and expressed his reasons for building the windmill. Then Napoleon stood up to reply. He said very quietly that the windmill was nonsense and that he advised nobody to vote for it and quickly sat down again. He spoke for nearly thirty seconds. At this Snowball jumped to his feet and began to talk in favour of the windmill. Until now the animals were equally divided in their sympathies. But in a moment Snowball's impressive speech carried them away. In his speech, he painted a picture of Animal Farm without hard work. Electricity, he said, could operate machines, ploughs, and harrows. Besides, it could supply every stall with its own electric light, hot and cold water, and an electric heater. There was no doubt now to which way the vote would go. But just at this moment Napoleon stood up and shouted very loudly. At this there was a terrible barking sound outside, and nine large dogs with brass collars came running into the barn. They ran straight for Snowball, who only jumped from his place just in time to escape their sharp jaws. In a moment he was out of the door and they were after him. Too surprised and frightened to speak, all the animals walked through the door to watch the chase. Snowball was running across the long pasture that led to the road. He was running as only a pig can run, but the dogs were close to him. Suddenly, Snowball began running faster than ever. But the dogs were very close to him again. One of them closed his jaws on Snowball's tail, but Snowball whisked it free just in time. Then he slipped through a hole in the hedge and disappeared. Silent and terrified, the animals crept back into the barn. In a moment the dogs came back. At first, no one could imagine where these creatures came from. But the problem was soon solved: they were the puppies whom Napoleon had taken away from their mothers and brought up privately. They were large dogs, and as fierce-looking as wolves. They kept close to Napoleon. They wagged their tails to him in the same way as other dogs had used to do to Mr Jones. Napoleon, with the dogs following him, came on to the raised portion of the floor. He said that from now on the Sunday-morning meetings would come to an end. They were unnecessary, he said, and wasted time. In future, all questions relating to the working of the farm would be settled by the pigs. These would meet in private and then communicate their decisions to the others. The animals would still gather on Sunday mornings to salute the flag, sing *the Beasts of England*, and receive their orders for the week. But there would be no more debates.

Despite their shock, the animals did not like this announcement. Several of them protested loudly. Even Boxer tried to protest this time. He set his ears back, shook his forelock several times, and tried hard to express his thoughts. But in the end, he could not think of anything to say. Some of the pigs themselves, however, were more articulate. Four young sheep in the front row jumped to their feet and began speaking at once. But suddenly the dogs sitting round Napoleon let out deep growls, and the sheep fell silent and sat down again. Then another sheep shouted, "Four legs good, two legs bad!" which went on for nearly a quarter of an hour and put an end to any chance of discussion. Soon Squealer explained the new rules to the others.

"Friends," he said, "I trust that every animal here respects a new leader on Animal Farm. Do not imagine, comrades, that leadership is an easy thing! On the contrary, it is a heavy responsibility. No one believes more firmly than Comrade Napoleon that all animals are equal. He would be only too happy to let you make your decisions for yourselves. But sometimes you can make the wrong decisions, my friends. Do you want to follow Snowball, with his nonsense of windmills – Snowball, who, as we now know, was no better than a criminal?"

"He fought bravely at the Battle of the Cowshed," said somebody.

"Bravery is not enough," said Squealer. "Loyalty and discipline are more important.Discipline, comrades, iron discipline! That is the rule for today. One false step and our enemies would conquer our farm. Surely, comrades, you do not want Jones back?"

Once again the animals did not protest. Of course, the animals did not want Jones back. Boxer, who had now enough time to think things over, finally said: "If Comrade Napoleon says so, it must be right." And this is how he found his new motto "Napoleon is always right" in addition to his private motto of "I will work harder."

By this time the winter was over and the spring ploughing began. Every Sunday morning at ten o'clock the animals gathered in the big barn to receive their orders for the week. Nowadays they did not sit all together as they had done in the past. Napoleon, with Squealer and another pig named Minimus, who could compose songs and poems, sat on the front of the raised platform, with the nine young dogs around them, and the other pigs sitting behind. The rest of the animals sat in the main body of the barn. Napoleon read out the orders for the week in a soldierly style and after a single singing of *the Beasts of England,* all the animals walked away.

On the third Sunday after Snowball's escape, the animals were somewhat surprised to hear that Napoleon wanted to build the windmill after all. He did not say why he changed his mind. However, he warned the animals that this extra task would mean hard work. Napoleon prepared the plans to the last detail. A special committee of pigs worked on them for the past three weeks. The building of the windmill would take two years. That evening Squealer explained to the other animals that Napoleon had never been against the windmill. On the contrary, it was Napoleon's idea in the beginning. Snowball stole the idea of the windmill from Napoleon's papers. The windmill was, in fact, Napoleon's creation.

"Why, then, did Napoleon speak so strongly against it?" said somebody.

Here Squealer looked cunning

"That was Comrade Napoleon's cunning. He SEEMED to oppose the windmill, simply to get rid of Snowball, who was a dangerous character. Now that Snowball is out of the way, the plan can go forward without his bad influence. This is something called tactics. Tactics, comrades, tactics!"

The animals were not sure what the word meant. Nevertheless, they accepted his explanation without further questions.

## Chapter 6

All that year the animals worked like slaves. But they were happy in their work. They knew well that everything that they did was for the benefit of themselves and those of their kind who would come after them, and not for human beings. Throughout the spring and summer, they worked a sixty-hour week. In August Napoleon announced that there would be work on Sunday afternoons as well. This work was voluntary, but he would reduce rations to any animal who absented himself from it. The animals did not make some important tasks that year because they worked hard on the windmill. The harvest was a little less successful than in the previous year. It was clear that the coming winter would be a hard one. The windmill presented unexpected difficulties. There was plenty of sand and cement on the farm. So all the building materials were at hand. But the problem the animals could not at first solve was how to break up the stone into pieces of suitable size. There seemed no way of doing this except with picks and crowbars, which no animal could use because no animal could stand on his hind legs. Only after weeks of vain efforts, the right idea occurred to some of the pigs. A pig proposed to use the force of gravity. The animals lashed ropes around large stones, and then all together, cows, horses, sheep, any animal that could take the rope, dragged them slowly to the top of the hill. Transporting the stone when it was once broken was quite simple. The horses carried it off in carts, the sheep dragged single blocks, even Muriel and Benjamin did their share.

By late summer, the animals collected large stones and then the building began, under the supervision of the pigs. But it was a slow, hard process. Often it took a whole day of hard work to drag a single stone to the top of the hill, and sometimes when it was pushed over the edge it failed to break. The animals could do nothing without Boxer, whose power seemed equal to that of all the rest of the animals put together. When the stone began to slip and the animals cried out in despair, it was always Boxer who pushed himself against the rope and brought the stone to a stop. Boxer's work filled everyone with admiration. Clover warned him sometimes to be careful not to hurt himself, but Boxer would never listen to her. His two slogans, "I will work harder" and Napoleon is always right" seemed to him a single answer to all his problems. And in his spare moments, of which there were not many nowadays, he would go alone to the hill, collect some broken stones, and drag them to the site of the windmill.

The animals were quite happy that summer, despite the hardness of their work. They did not have less than they had had in Jones's day. They worked to feed themselves, not cruel human beings. And, in many ways, the animal method of doing things was more effective. Such jobs as weeding, for example, could be done with care impossible to human beings. Nevertheless, as the summer went on, the animals faced different shortages on the farm. There was need of paraffin oil, nails, rope, dog biscuits, and iron for the horses' shoes. The animals could produce none of them on the farm. There was also a need for seeds and tools and, finally, the machinery for the windmill. No one knew how to produce or find all these things.

One Sunday morning, when the animals gathered to receive their orders, Napoleon announced that he had decided to engage in trade with the neighbouring farms. Not, of course, for money, but simply to gain some necessary materials. The needs of the windmill must override everything else, he said. That is why he was making arrangements to sell a stack of hay and part of a wheat crop, and later on, eggs, for which there was always a market in Willingdon. The hens, said Napoleon, must welcome this sacrifice as their special contribution towards the building of the windmill. Once again the animals recalled the Seven Commandments – Never to engage in trade and never to use money. All the animals remembered this commandment, or at least they thought that they remembered it. The four young sheep began to protest, but they were quickly silenced by a loud growling from the dogs. Then another sheep said, "Four legs good, two legs bad!" and the protest was over. Finally, Napoleon raised his trotter for silence and announced that he had already made all the arrangements. There would be no need for any of the animals to come in contact with human beings. Napoleon wanted to engage in trade with human beings all by himself. Mr Whymper, a farmer living in Willingdon, agreed to visit Animal Farm on Monday morning. Napoleon ended his speech with his usual cry of "Long live Animal Farm!" After the singing of *the Beasts of England,* Napoleon went away silently. His dogs followed him. Squealer assured the animals that there was nothing wrong in trade and money. Napoleon must engage in trade with human beings simply to gain the necessary materials for Animal Farm. A few animals still felt doubtful. Some of them recalled the Seven Commandments. Squealer asked them at once:

"Are you sure that this is not something that you have dreamed, comrades? Have you any record of such commandments? Is it written down anywhere?"

The animals did not say a word. They were frightened to talk about the Seven Commandments.

On Monday morning, Mr Whymper visited Animal Farm. He was a little man with side whiskers. He was a solicitor in a very small way of business. The animals watched his coming and going with fear. They avoided him as much as possible. Nevertheless, the sight of Napoleon, on four legs, giving orders to Mr Whymper, who stood on two legs, roused their pride considerably. Their relations with human beings were now not quite the same as they had been before. But human beings still hated Animal Farm more than ever. Every human being was sure that the farm would go bankrupt sooner or later, and that the windmill would be a failure. They would meet in their houses and prove to one another using diagrams that the windmill would fail. And yet, against their will, they were surprised at how animals were managing their farm. They began to call Animal Farm by its proper name and stopped to pretend that it was called the Manor Farm. They also did not meet with Jones, who had given up hope of getting his farm back and gone to live in another part of the county. Apart from Mr Whymper, there was no contact between Animal Farm and the outside world. However, there were constant rumours that Napoleon engaged in trade with Mr Pilkington of Foxwood or with Mr Frederick of Pinchfield. But nobody noticed Napoleon with both farmers.

It was about this time that the pigs suddenly moved into the farmhouse and started to live there. Again the animals recalled the Seven Commandments, and again Squealer convinced them that this was not the case. It was necessary, he said, that the pigs, who were the brains of the farm, must have a quiet place to work in. It was also more suitable for the Leader (Napoleon, of course) to live in a house than a stall. Nevertheless, some of the animals were surprised when they heard that the pigs not only took their meals in the kitchen but also slept in the beds. Boxer expressed his opinion as usual with "Napoleon is always right!", but Clover, who thought she remembered a commandment against beds, went to the barn and tried to read the Seven Commandments which were written there. When she could not read them at all, she sent for Muriel.

"Muriel," she said, "read me the Fourth Commandment. Does it not say something about never sleeping in a bed?"

With some difficulty, Muriel spelt it out.

"It says, 'No animal shall sleep in a bed with sheets,'" said Muriel.

Clover had not remembered that the Fourth Commandment mentioned sheets; but as it was there on the wall, it must be correct. And Squealer, who was passing at this moment with three dogs, explained the whole matter in his own way.

"You have heard then, comrades," he said, "that we pigs now sleep in the beds of the farmhouse? And why not? You do not think, surely, that there was ever a rule against beds? A bed means a place to sleep in. A pile of straw in a stall is a bed too. The rule was against sheets, which are human invention. We have removed the sheets from the farmhouse beds, and sleep between blankets. And they are very comfortable beds! But not more comfortable than we need, I can tell you, comrades, with all the brainwork we have to do nowadays. You would not say something against this, would you, comrades? You would not have us too tired to carry out our duties? Surely none of you wishes to see Jones back?"

The animals reassured him on this point at once. No more was said about the pigs sleeping in the farmhouse beds. And when, after two days, it was announced that from now on the pigs would get up an hour later in the mornings than the other animals, the animals made no complaint about that either.

By the autumn the animals were tired but happy. They had had a hard year, and after the sale of the hay and corn, the stores of food for the winter were quite small, but the windmill compensated for everything. It was almost half built now. After the harvest, the animals worked harder than ever. Boxer even came out at nights and worked for an hour or two alone. In their spare moments, the animals walked round the half-finished mill, admiring the power of its walls. Only old Benjamin was not enthusiastic about the windmill. As usual, he said nothing beyond the remark that donkeys live a long time. November came, with cold south-west winds. The building had to stop because it was now too wet to mix the cement. One night, the wind was so violent that the farm buildings rocked on their foundations. The hens woke up with roar because they had all seemed to hear a gun firing in the distance. In the morning, the animals came out of their stalls carefully. The next moment a cry of despair broke from every animal's throat. They saw a terrible sight. The windmill was in ruins. They all ran towards it. Napoleon ran ahead of them all. Yes, there it lay, the result of all their struggles. The stones were scattered all around. The animals could not speak. They stood looking sadly at the ruins of the windmill. Napoleon walked to and fro in silence, sometimes snuffing at the ground. His tail moved sharply from side to side. He was very thoughtful. Suddenly, he stopped and looked at the animals seriously.

"Comrades," he said, "do you know who is responsible for this? Do you know the enemy who came in the night and destroyed our windmill! Snowball! It was Snowball!" Snowball did this thing! This traitor crept here at night and destroyed our work of a year. Comrades, here and now I pronounce the death sentence on Snowball. 'Animal Hero, Second Class,' and a basket of apples to any animal who catches him alive!"

The animals were shocked to learn that Snowball was guilty of such an action. There was a cry of despair, and everyone began thinking out ways of catching. Almost immediately Napoleon discovered Snowball's footprints in the grass at a little distance from the barn. The footprints seemed to lead to a hole in the hedge. Napoleon snuffed deeply at them. They belonged to Snowball without a doubt. Napoleon said that Snowball came from the direction of Foxwood Farm.

"No more delays, comrades!" cried Napoleon. "There is work to be done. This very morning, we begin rebuilding the windmill. We will build it! We will teach this miserable traitor that he cannot destroy our work so easily. Remember, comrades, there must be no change in our plans. Forward, comrades! Long live the windmill! Long live Animal Farm!"

## Chapter 7

It was a cold winter. The stormy weather was followed by sleet and snow. A hard frost did not break till February. The animals worked as best they could to rebuild the windmill quickly. They knew well that the outside world was watching them. They were doing their best to finish the windmill on time. The human beings pretended not to believe that it was Snowball who had destroyed the windmill. They said that it had fallen because the walls were too thin. The animals knew that this was not true. Still, Napoleon decided to build the walls thicker this time, which meant collecting much larger stones. For a long time, the hill was full of snowdrifts and nothing could be done. Some progress was made in the dry frosty weather, but it was hard work, and the animals felt helpless and distressed. They were always cold, and usually hungry as well. Only Boxer and Clover never lost heart. Squealer made excellent speeches on the joy of service and the dignity of hard work. However, the animals found more inspiration in Boxer's power and his motto of "I will work harder!"

In January food fell short. The corn ration was dramatically reduced. Squealer announced that the animals would receive an extra potato ration on weekends. Then the animals discovered that the greater part of the potato had been frosted in the store. It had not been covered thickly enough. The potatoes had become soft and spoilt, and only a few were good. For many days, the animals had nothing to eat but chaff. Starvation seemed to look them in the face. It was necessary to hide this fact from the outside world. The human beings invented fresh lies about Animal Farm. They said that all the animals were dying of starvation and disease, and that they were fighting among themselves all the time. Napoleon did his best to stop the rumours about Animal Farm. He decided to make use of Mr Whymper to spread a good impression. The animals had no contact with Mr Whymper. So Napoleon ordered a few pigs to fill empty bins in the store nearly to the brim with sand. After that, he ordered them to cover it up with what remained of the grain and meal. One day, Napoleon led Mr Whymper through the store and asked him to look at the full bins. Mr Whymper did not believe Napoleon. He continued to report to the outside world that there was no food shortage on Animal Farm. Nevertheless, towards the end of January, it became clear that it would be necessary to buy more grain from somewhere. In these days Napoleon seldom came to the barn. He spent all his time in the farmhouse, which was guarded at each door by large dogs. When he did come to the barn, it was in a ceremonial style, with an escort of six dogs who surrounded him and growled if anyone came too near. Soon he did not even come to the barn on Sunday mornings. He gave his orders through one of the other pigs, usually Squealer.

One Sunday morning, Squealer announced that the hens must surrender their eggs. Napoleon wanted to sell four hundred eggs every week. The price of these eggs would pay for enough grain and meal to keep the farm going till summer came on. When the hens heard this, they began to protest terribly. They were just getting their eggs ready for the spring sitting. They said that to take the eggs away now was murder. For the first time since the escape of Jones, there was something resembling a rebellion. The hens refused to give their eggs to Napoleon. Napoleon acted quickly. He ordered to stop the hen's ration. For five days the hens did not eat grain. Some of them capitulated and went back to their nesting boxes. Nine hens died of hunger. Napoleon sold their bodies to Mr Whymper. The other hens agreed to give their eggs away every week. A grocer's van drove up to the farm once a week to take the eggs away.

All this time nothing was heard of Snowball. Napoleon said that he was hiding on one of the neighbouring farms, either Foxwood or Pinchfield. Napoleon was by this time on better terms with the other farmers than before. There was a pile of timber in the yard. Mr Whymper advised Napoleon to sell it. Both Mr Pilkington and Mr Frederick wanted to buy it. Napoleon was hesitating between the two farmers. He could not make up his mind. One day, early in the spring, Napoleon discovered a terrible thing. Snowball came secretly to Animal Farm the previous night! The animals were so scared that they could hardly sleep in their stalls. Every night, Napoleon said, Snowball came to the farm to make all kinds of mischief. He stole the corn, he drank the milk, he broke the eggs, he destroyed the seeds, he broke the fruit trees and so on. Whenever anything went wrong, Snowball was always guilty. If a window was broken, someone said that Snowball had come in the night and done it. When the key of the store was lost, the whole farm was sure that Snowball had thrown it down the well. The cows once said that Snowball crept into their stalls and milked them in their sleep. The rats, which were very troublesome that winter, were also in league with Snowball. Napoleon and his dogs made a careful tour of inspection of the farm buildings, the other animals following at a distance. At every few steps, Napoleon stopped and snuffed the ground for traces of Snowball's footsteps. Napoleon could detect Snowball's footsteps even by the smell. He snuffed in every corner, in the barn, in the cow-shed, in the henhouses, in the vegetable garden, and found traces of Snowball almost everywhere.

"Snowball! He has been here! I can smell him here!" said Napoleon.

And at the word "Snowball" all the dogs growled loudly and showed their sharp teeth. The animals were very frightened. It seemed to them that Snowball was the most dangerous enemy of Animal Farm. One evening, Squealer called them together and told them that he had some serious news to report.

"Comrades!" cried Squealer, "a most terrible thing has been discovered. Snowball has sold himself to Frederick of Pinchfield Farm! He is planning to attack us and take our farm away from us! Snowball will act as Frederick's guide when the attack begins. But there is worse than that. We always thought that Snowball had caused a rebellion because of his ambitions. But we were wrong, comrades. Do you know what the real reason was? Snowball was in league with Jones from the very start! He was Jones's secret agent all the time. Napoleon learned this from the documents which Snowball had left behind him. This explains a great deal, comrades. Do you understand how he tried to get us destroyed at the Battle of the Cowshed?"

The animals were shocked. But it was some minutes before they could say a word. They all remembered or thought they remembered, how they had seen Snowball running ahead of them at the Battle of the Cowshed and how he encouraged them to fight against human beings. At first, it was difficult for the animals to understand how Snowball was on Jones's side. Even Boxer, who seldom asked questions, was confused. He lay down, shut his eyes, and tried to formulate his thoughts. A few minutes passed.

"I do not believe that," he said. "Snowball fought bravely at the Battle of the Cowshed. I saw him myself. Did we not give him 'Animal Hero, First Class,' immediately after the battle?"

"That was our mistake," said Squealer. "We know the truth now, comrade. It is all written down in the secret documents that we have found. In reality, he was trying to destroy Animal Farm."

"But he had wounds," said Boxer.

"That was part of the arrangement!" cried Squealer. Jones's shot only wounded him. Snowball gave the signal for retreat and left the field to the enemy. He failed thanks to our heroic Leader, Comrade Napoleon. Do you not remember how, just at the moment when Jones and his men had got inside the yard, Snowball suddenly turned and ran away, and many animals followed him? And do you not remember that it was just at that moment, when all seemed lost, that Comrade Napoleon jumped forward and sank his teeth in Jones's leg? Surely you remember THAT, comrades?"

Now when Squealer described the scene so well, it seemed to the animals that they remembered it. But Boxer still had some doubts.

"I do not believe that Snowball was a traitor at the beginning," he said finally. "What he has done after his escape is different. But I believe that at the Battle of the Cowshed he was a good comrade."

"Our Leader, Comrade Napoleon," announced Squealer, speaking very slowly and firmly, "had said that Snowball was Jones's agent from the very beginning. If he says so, then it is true."

"Ah, that is different!" said Boxer. "If Comrade Napoleon says it, it must be right.

"That is true, comrade!" cried Squealer.

Squealer turned to go, then stopped and said angrily:

"I warn every animal on this farm to keep his eyes wide open. For we have reason to think that some of Snowball's secret agents are among us at this moment!"

Four days later, in the late afternoon, Napoleon ordered all the animals to gather in the yard. When they were all gathered together, Napoleon came from the farmhouse, wearing both his medals ("Animal Hero, First Class", and "Animal Hero, Second Class"), with his nine huge dogs walking around him. All the animals stood silently in their places. They were very scared. Napoleon looked at them angrily. Then he cried loudly and looked at his dogs. Immediately the dogs stepped forward, seized four of the sheep by the ear and dragged them to Napoleon's feet. The sheep's ears were bleeding. The four sheep waited, trembling with fear. Napoleon now ordered them to confess their crimes. They confessed that they had been secretly in league with Snowball ever since his escape, that they had helped him in destroying the windmill, and that they planned to hand over Animal Farm to Mr Frederick. When they finished their confession, the dogs quickly tore their throats out, and, in a terrible voice, Napoleon asked whether any other animal had anything to confess. The three hens came forward and said that Snowball had ordered them to kill Napoleon. The dogs killed them too. Then a goose came forward and confessed as well. He had taken six ears of corn during the last year's harvest and eaten them at night. They were all killed at once. The confessions and executions continued until there was a pile of corpses lying before Napoleon's feet and the air was heavy with the smell of blood. When it was all over, the remaining animals, except for the pigs and dogs, crept away to the barn. They were frightened and miserable. They did not know which was more shocking – the treachery of the animals or the cruel executions. In the old days, there had often been scenes of bloodshed, but it seemed to all of them that it was far worse now because it was happening among themselves. Until today, no animal had killed another animal. Not even a rat had been killed. When they came into the barn, they all lay down silently – Clover, Muriel, Benjamin, the cows, the sheep, and a whole flock of geese and hens. Everyone lay down, except the cat, who had suddenly disappeared just before Napoleon ordered the animals to gather before him. For some time nobody spoke. Only Boxer remained on his feet. He walked to and fro, moving his long black tail. Finally, he said seriously:

"I do not understand it. I would not have believed that such things could happen on our farm. We have made some mistakes. The solution, as I see it, is to work harder. From now on, I will get up an hour earlier in the mornings."

And he walked away to the hill. There he collected two large stones and dragged them down to the windmill. He worked alone. Then Clover went to the hill and joined Boxer in his work. The other animals gathered about Clover, not speaking. The hill where they were standing gave them a wide view across the countryside – the long pasture stretching down to the main road, the hayfield, the drinking pool, the ploughed fields where the young wheat was thick and green, and the red roofs of the farm buildings. It was a clear spring evening. With a kind of surprise, they remembered that it was their farm. Animal Farm never seemed to the animals such a good place. As Clover looked down the hillside her eyes filled with tears. She could not speak her thoughts. She was scared. These scenes of terror and murder were wrong. The Rebellion had not described such terrible things. It had described the future, where all the animals were equal, where they were free from hunger and the whip, each working according to his capacity, the strong protecting the weak… She did not know why they had come to a time when no one dared to speak, when growling dogs walked everywhere, and when you had to watch your friends torn to pieces after confessing to shocking crimes. There was no thought of rebellion or disobedience in her mind. She knew that they had a better life than they had in the days of Jones, and that it was necessary to prevent the return of human beings. Whatever happened she would remain faithful, work hard, and accept the leadership of Napoleon. But still, it was not for this that she and all the other animals had hoped and worked. It was not for this that they had built the windmill and faced the bullets of Jones's gun. Such were her thoughts, but she could not express them. At last, she began to sing *the Beasts of England*. The other animals sitting round her began to sing too. They all sang it slowly and mournfully, in a way they had never sung it before. At that moment Squealer and two dogs came up to them. They were angry.

"Comrade Napoleon forbade you to sing *the Beasts of England*!" said Squealer.

The animals were surprised to hear that.

"Why?" cried Muriel.

"It is not necessary anymore, comrade," said Squealer. "*The Beasts of England* was the song of the Rebellion. But the Rebellion is now finished. The execution of the traitors this afternoon was the final act. Our enemies were defeated. In *the Beasts of England,* we expressed our desire for a better society in the future. We established such society long ago. This song has no longer any purpose."

The animals were too scared to say a word. The cruel growling of the dogs put end to the discussion. The animals never sang *the Beasts of England.* Instead of *the Beasts of England* Minimus, the poet, composed another song which began:

*Animal Farm, Animal Farm,*
*In this place we will never come to harm!*

The animals sang this song every Sunday morning after the hoisting of the flag.

## Chapter 8

A few days later, the animals did not forget the terror caused by the executions. Some of the animals remembered the Sixth Commandment “No animal will kill any other animal.” No one cared to mention it in the presence of the pigs or the dogs. Clover asked Benjamin to read her the Sixth Commandment. Benjamin read the Commandment for her. It ran:

“No animal will kill any other animal WITHOUT CAUSE.”

Somehow or other, Clover could not remember the last two words. But they saw now that the Commandment was not violated. There was good reason for killing the traitors who had leagued themselves with Snowball.

Throughout the year the animals worked even harder than they had worked in the previous year. It was very difficult to rebuild the windmill, with walls twice as thick as before, and to finish it on time, together with the regular work of the farm. There were times when it seemed to the animals that they worked longer hours and fed no better than they had done in Jones’s day. On Sunday mornings Squealer, holding a long paper with his trotter, read out to them lists of figures proving that the production of food had increased greatly. The animals believed him because they could no longer remember very clearly how they had lived before the Rebellion. Nevertheless, they wanted less figures and more food. Squealer or one of the other pigs gave orders to the animals on Animal Farm. Napoleon came to the barn once or twice a month. His large dogs always followed him. Even in the farmhouse Napoleon lived in separate apartments from the others. He took his meals alone, with two dogs next to him. He always ate from the dinner service which had been in the glass cupboard in the drawing-room. The animals now never call him simply "Napoleon. They always called him in formal style as "our Leader, Comrade Napoleon," and the pigs invented for him such titles as Father of All Animals, Terror of Mankind, Protector of the Sheep-fold, Ducklings' Friend, and the like. In his speeches, Squealer would talk with the tears rolling down his cheeks about Napoleon's wisdom and the kindness of his heart, and the deep love he felt to all animals everywhere, even and especially the unhappy animals who still lived in slavery on other farms. It had become usual to give Napoleon the credit for every successful thing on the farm. One day, a hen said to another, "Under the guidance of our Leader, Comrade Napoleon, I have laid five eggs in six days". Another day, two cows, enjoying a drink at the pool, said, "Thanks to the leadership of Comrade Napoleon, how excellent this water tastes!" The general feeling on the farm was well expressed in the poem "Comrade Napoleon." Minimus devoted his poem to Napoleon, of course. The poem ran as follows:

*Friend of all animals!*
*Fountain of happiness!*
*My soul is on fire*
*When I look at your*
*Calm and commanding eye.*
*Like the sun in the sky,*
*Comrade Napoleon!*

*You are the giver of*
*All that your creatures love,*
*Full belly twice a day, clean stall to sleep upon,*
*Every animal, big or small,*
*Sleeps at peace in his stall,*
*You watch over all,*
*Comrade Napoleon!*
*A new-born animal*
*Should learn to be faithful to you,*
*Yes, his first word should be*
*"Comrade Napoleon!"*

Napoleon liked this poem and ordered to write it on the wall of the barn, at the opposite side from the Seven Commandments. Squealer painted a portrait of Napoleon, in profile, near the poem as well.

At that time, Napoleon was engaged in negotiations with Frederick and Pilkington. The pile of timber was still unsold. Frederick and Pilkington did not offer a good price. Napoleon still hesitated. At the same time, there were fresh rumours that Frederick and his men were planning to attack Animal Farm and to destroy the windmill. The windmill aroused furious jealousy in him. Napoleon said that Snowball was still living on Pinchfield Farm. In the middle of the summer, three hens came forward and confessed that, inspired by Snowball, they planned to kill Napoleon. They were killed immediately. Napoleon took some precautions at once. Four dogs guarded his bed at night, one at each corner and a young pig named Pinkeye tasted all his food before he ate it. At about the same time Napoleon arranged to sell the pile of timber to

Mr Pilkington. Napoleon was also going to exchange some products between Animal Farm and Foxwood. The relations between Napoleon and Pilkington were now almost friendly. The animals distrusted Pilkington, as a human being.

In the summer the windmill was almost ready. The rumours about the attack grew stronger and stronger. Frederick, it was said, wanted to bring twenty men with guns. Moreover, terrible stories were circulating out from Pinchfield about the cruelties that Frederick practised on his animals. He overworked his old horse to death, he starved his cows, he killed a dog, he amused himself in the evenings by making cocks fights. The animals' blood boiled with anger when they heard of these things. Sometimes they wanted to go out and attack Pinchfield Farm, drive out the humans, and set the animals free. But Squealer forbade them to do that. He ordered them to trust Comrade Napoleon's strategy. Nevertheless, feeling against Frederick continued to run high. One Sunday morning, Napoleon came to the barn and explained that he had never wanted to sell the pile of timber to Frederick. He ordered the pigeons, who were still spreading news of the Rebellion, to say "Death to Frederick" when they flew over Foxwood.

In the late summer, Napoleon discovered more of Snowball's mischief. The wheat crop was full of weeds. Napoleon discovered that Snowball had mixed weed seeds with the corn seeds. The animals now also learned that Snowball had never received "Animal Hero, First Class." This was just a legend which had been spread sometime after the Battle of the Cowshed by Snowball himself. Once again some of the animals heard this with surprise, but Squealer quickly convinced them that their memories had been wrong.

In the autumn, the windmill was finished. The animals had to install the machinery for the windmill. Napoleon was negotiating with Mr Whymper to get the best price. Anyway, the structure was completed. Despite inexperience, primitive tools, bad luck and Snowball's treachery, the animals finished the windmill on time! Tired but proud, the animals walked round and round their masterpiece. The windmill seemed to be even more beautiful in their eyes than the first windmill which had been destroyed by Snowball. The walls were twice as thick as before. Nothing and nobody could destroy it this time! And when they thought of how they had worked, they forgot their tiredness and they walked round and round the windmill gladly. Napoleon himself, attended by his dogs, came down to see the windmill. He congratulated the animals on their achievement and named the windmill Napoleon Mill.

Two days later, Squealer called the animals together for a special meeting in the barn. They were very surprised when Napoleon announced that he had sold the pile of timber to Frederick. Tomorrow Frederick's wagons would arrive and begin carting it away. Throughout the whole period of his friendship with Pilkington, Napoleon was in secret agreement with Frederick. All relations with Foxwood were finished once and for all. Napoleon ordered the pigeons to avoid Pinchfield Farm and to change their slogan from "Death to Frederick" to "Death to Pilkington." At the same time, Napoleon assured the animals that the stories of an attack on Animal Farm were untrue and that the tales about Frederick's cruelty to his animals had been exaggerated. All these rumours had probably originated with Snowball and his agents. It now seemed that Snowball was not hiding on Pinchfield Farm. In fact, he was living in luxury at Foxwood Farm and was an agent of Pilkington for years past. The pigs admired Napoleon's cunning. He forced Frederick to raise his price by twelve pounds. He trusted nobody, not even Frederick. Frederick wanted to pay for the timber with something called a cheque. It was a piece of paper. But Napoleon was too clever for him. He wanted payment in real five-pound notes. Frederick had already paid up, and the sum he had paid was just enough to buy the machinery for the windmill. Frederick carted away the timber very quickly. When it was all gone, another special meeting was held in the barn for the animals to inspect Frederick's bank-notes. Napoleon was very proud of himself. He lay on a bed of straw on the platform, with his money at his side. The animals looked at the bank-notes attentively. Boxer put out his nose to sniff at the bank-notes, and the white things moved in his breath.

Three days later there was a terrible discovery. The animals heard a roar from Napoleon's apartments. The news of what had happened spread round the farm like wildfire. The banknotes were not real! Frederick had got the timber for nothing! Napoleon called the animals together immediately and in a terrible voice pronounced the death sentence on Frederick. At the same time, he warned them that Frederick and his men might make their attack at any moment. Napoleon placed his guards at all the corners of the farmhouse. He sent four pigeons to Foxwood with a message, which would establish good relations with Pilkington. The next morning the attack came. The animals were at breakfast when the pigeons came flying in with the news that Frederick and his men had already come through the gate. The animals ran to the gate to meet them. This time they did not have the easy victory that they had had in the

Battle of the Cowshed. There were fifteen men, with guns, and they opened fire as soon as they got within fifty yards. The animals could not face terrible bullets. Despite the efforts of Napoleon and Boxer to stop the men, the animals had to retreat soon. A number of them were already wounded. They ran to the farm buildings and looked carefully out from windows and knot-holes. The whole of the big pasture, including the windmill, was in the hands of the enemy. For the moment even Napoleon seemed frightened. He walked up and down without a word. He looked very angry. Nothing and nobody could help them now. At that moment Frederick and his men stopped about the windmill. The animals watched them, and a cry of dismay went round. Two of the men took a crowbar and a hammer. They were going to destroy the windmill!

"Impossible!" cried Napoleon. "The walls are too thick for that. They cannot destroy it. Courage, comrades!"

But Benjamin was watching the movements of the men attentively. The two with the hammer and the crowbar were drilling a hole near the base of the windmill.

"I thought so," he said. "Do you not see what they are doing? In another moment they are going to pack a powder into that hole."

Terrified, the animals waited. It was impossible now to come out of the shelter of the buildings. After a few minutes, the men were running in all directions. Then there was a loud noise. The pigeons flew into the air, and all the animals, except Napoleon, lay flat on their bellies and hid their faces. When they got up again, a huge cloud of black smoke was hanging over the windmill. Slowly the wind drifted it away. The windmill was destroyed! At this sight, the animals' courage returned to them. The fear and despair they had felt a moment earlier were gone in their anger against the cruel men. They cried madly. Without waiting for further orders, they ran straight for the enemy. This time they were not afraid of the bullets that swept over them like hail. It was a bitter battle. The men fired again and again, and the animals got close to them. The men tried to hurt the animals with their sticks and heavy boots. A cow, three sheep, and two geese were killed, and almost everyone was wounded. Even Napoleon, who was giving orders, had the tip of his tail chipped by a pellet. But the men were wounded too. Three of them had their heads broken by blows from Boxer's hoofs, another had their trousers torn off by Jessie and Bluebell. Then the nine dogs of Napoleon's bodyguard suddenly attacked the men from the hedge. The men were in a panic. They saw that they were in danger. Frederick shouted to his men to run away. The next moment the enemy was running for dear life. The animals chased them right down to the bottom of the field, as they made their way through the hedge. The animals won, but they were tired and wounded. Slowly they began to limp back towards the farm. They cried over their dead comrades who lay on the grass. For a little while, they stopped in silence at the place where the windmill had once stood. Yes, it was gone! Even the foundations were destroyed. They could not rebuild it this time. This time the stones were destroyed too. The explosion scattered the stones in all directions. As they came back to the barn, Squealer, who had been absent during the fighting, came running towards them. He looked quite happy. But the animals heard, from the direction of the farm buildings, the firing of a gun.

"What is that gun firing for?" said Boxer.

"To celebrate our victory!" cried Squealer.

"What victory?" said Boxer.

His knees were bleeding, he had lost a shoe during the battle. He had a bullet in his hind leg.

"What victory, comrade? Have we not won the battle?"

"But they have destroyed the windmill. And we had worked on it for two years!"

"What matter? We will build another windmill. We will build six windmills! We have done a great thing! Thanks to the leadership of Comrade Napoleon, we have won again!"

"Then we have won back what we had before," said Boxer.

"That is our victory," said Squealer.

The animals walked slowly into the yard. The bullet under the skin of Boxer's leg caused him pain. He saw ahead of him the heavy work of rebuilding the windmill from the foundations, and already he prepared himself for the task. For the first time, it occurred to him that he was eleven years old and that perhaps his muscles were not good for such a difficult task. But when the animals saw the green flag flying, heard the gun firing again, and heard the speech that Napoleon made, congratulating them on their victory, it seemed to them after all they had won a great victory. They buried the dead animals. Napoleon himself walked at the head of the procession. Two whole days were given over to celebrations. There were songs, speeches, and more firing of the gun, and a special gift of an apple for every animal, and a plate of corn for each bird and three biscuits for each dog. It was announced that the battle would be called the Battle of the Windmill. Napoleon created a new decoration – the Order of the Green Banner, which he gave to himself. In the general celebrations, the false banknotes were forgotten. It was a few days later when the pigs found a case of whisky in the cellars of the farmhouse.That night there came from the farmhouse the sound of loud singing, in which, to everyone's surprise, the words of *the Beasts of England* were mixed up. At about half-past nine Napoleon, wearing an old hat of Mr Jones's, came from the back door, walked quickly around the yard, and disappeared indoors again. But in the morning there was a deep silence in the farmhouse. Not a pig came out of the farmhouse. It was nearly nine o'clock when Squealer came out, walking slowly in the yard. His eyes were red. He looked seriously ill. He called the animals together and told them that he had terrible news to say. Comrade Napoleon was dying! There was a cry of surprise. The animals began to cry bitterly. With tears in their eyes, they asked one another what they should do if their Leader died. A rumour went round that Snowball had mixed some poison into Napoleon's food. At eleven o'clock Squealer came out to make another announcement. Comrade Napoleon gave another order to the animals: the animals were not allowed to drink the alcohol. By the evening, however, Napoleon seemed to be somewhat better. The following morning Squealer told the animals that he was well on the way to recovery. By the evening of that day, Napoleon was back at work, and on the next day it was learned that he had asked Whymper to buy in Willingdon some booklets on brewing and distilling. Soon the animals learned that Napoleon wanted to sow it with barley.

About this time a strange incident happened which nobody could understand. One night at about midnight, there was a loud crash in the yard, and the animals ran out of their stalls. At the foot of the end wall of the barn, where the Seven Commandments were written, there lay a ladder broken in two pieces. Squealer lay beside it. There lay a lantern, a paint-brush, and an overturned pot of white paint next to him. The dogs immediately made a ring round Squealer. He went back to the farmhouse as soon as he could walk. None of the animals could form any idea as to what this meant, except old Benjamin, who seemed to understand everything. But he said nothing at all. A few days later Muriel read over the Seven Commandments to herself. She noticed that there was another of them which the animals had remembered wrong. They had thought the Fifth Commandment was "No animal shall drink alcohol," but there were two words that they had forgotten. In reality, the Commandment was: "No animal shall drink alcohol TOO MUCH."

## Chapter 9

Boxer's hind leg still ached a lot. They had started the rebuilding of the windmill the day after the victory celebrations had ended. Boxer refused to take even a day off work and tried to hide the fact that he was in pain. In the evenings he would say privately to Clover that the leg troubled him all the time. Clover treated his leg with herbs which she prepared by chewing them. Both she and Benjamin asked Boxer to work less hard. "A horse's legs do not last forever," she said to him. But Boxer would not listen. He had, he said, only one wish left – to see the windmill before he reached the age for retirement. In the beginning, when the laws of Animal Farm were first formulated, the retiring age for horses and pigs were at twelve, for cows at fourteen, for dogs at nine, for sheep at seven, and for hens and geese at five. Yet no animal had actually retired on pension. However, the animals discussed this subject more and more. For a horse, it was said, the pension would be five pounds of corn a day and, in winter, fifteen pounds of hay, with a carrot or an apple on public holidays. Boxer's twelfth birthday would be in the late summer of the following year.

Meanwhile life was hard. The winter was very cold and the food was even shorter. Once again all rations were reduced, except those of the pigs and the dogs. Squealer explained that too much food was contrary to the principles of Animalism. He had no difficulty in proving to the other animals that they were NOT short of food. It was necessary to reduce rations, but in comparison with the days of Jones, the improvement was great. By reading out the figures on a piece of paper, he proved to them in detail that they had more oats, more hay, more apples than they had had in Jones's day, that they worked shorter hours, that their drinking water was of better quality, that they lived longer, and that they had more straw in their stalls and suffered less from fleas. The animals believed every word of it. In fact, they knew that life nowadays was hard, that they were often hungry and often cold, and that they were usually working when they were not asleep. But, doubtless, it had been worse in the old days. They were glad to believe so. Besides, in those days they had been slaves and now they were free, and that made all the difference.

There were many more mouths to feed now. In the autumn the four sows gave birth to thirty-one young pigs. As Napoleon was the only boar on the farm, it was possible to guess at their parentage. Napoleon ordered to build a schoolroom for the young pigs in the farmhouse garden. Napoleon forbade them to play with the other young animals. About this time, Napoleon announced the new rule: when a pig and any other animal met on the path, the other animal must stand aside. Besides this, all the pigs could wear green ribbons on their tails on Sundays. The farm had quite a successful year, but was still short of money. There were not enough bricks, sand, and stones for the schoolroom. It was also necessary to begin saving up again for the machinery for the windmill. They needed lamp oil and candles for the house, sugar for Napoleon's table (he forbade this to the other pigs because it made them fat), and all the usual tools, nails, string, coal, wire, and dog biscuits. Napoleon sold a stump of hay and part of the potato crop. He increased the contract for eggs to six hundred a week. So that year the hens could not have enough chicks to keep their numbers at the same level. Rations, reduced in December, were reduced again in February. Lanterns in the stalls were forbidden to save oil. But the pigs seemed comfortable enough and were putting on weight.

One afternoon in late February, the animals felt a delicious scent across the yard from the little brew-house, which stood beyond the kitchen. Someone said it was the smell of cooking barley. The animals sniffed the air hungrily and wondered whether they would have warm barley for their supper. They did not eat warm barley that day. On the following Sunday, it was announced that all barley would be reserved for the pigs. The field beyond the orchard had already been sown with barley. Soon the animals learned that every pig was now receiving a glass of beer daily.

Their life nowadays had a greater dignity than it had had before. There were more songs, more speeches, more ceremonies. Once a week they held something called a Spontaneous Demonstration, the object of which was to celebrate the struggles and triumphs of Animal Farm. The animals left their work and walk around the farm in military style, with the pigs leading, then the horses, then the cows, then the sheep, and then the hens. The dogs guarded the ceremony. Napoleon walked at the head of all. Boxer and Clover always carried between them a green banner marked with the hoof and the horn and the caption, "Long live Comrade Napoleon!" After that, the pigs read the poems composed in Napoleon's honour. Then Squealer read aloud to them the latest increases in the production of food, and on occasion a shot was fired from the gun. The sheep liked the Spontaneous Demonstration most of all. If anyone complained (as a few animals sometimes did, when no pigs or dogs were near), the sheep silenced him with their usual phrase, "Four legs good, two legs bad!" But the animals enjoyed these celebrations. The celebrations reminded them that, after all, they were truly their own masters and that the work they did was for their benefit. Thanks to the songs, the processions, Squealer's lists of figures, the firing of the gun, and the fluttering of the flag, they could forget that their bellies were empty.

In April, Animal Farm was proclaimed a Republic, and it became necessary to elect a President. There was only one candidate – Napoleon. The pigs elected him immediately. On the same day, the pigs found fresh documents which revealed further details about Snowball's friendship with Jones. Squealer explained to the animals all the details of Snowball's treachery. The animals believed him without saying a word. In the middle of the summer, Moses the raven suddenly came back to the farm, after an absence of several years. He was quite unchanged. He still did not work and talked in the same way as ever about Sugarcandy Mountain. He talked to anyone who would listen.

"Up there, comrades," he said, pointing to the sky with his large wing, "up there, just on the other side of that dark cloud that you can see. There it lies, Sugarcandy Mountain, that happy country where we poor animals will rest forever from our hard work!"

He even has been there on one of his higher flights and has seen the endless fields of clover and the lump sugar growing on the hedges. Many of the animals believed him. Their lives were now hungry and hard. Was it not right that a better world should exist somewhere else? The pigs did not like Moses's stories. They all said that his stories about Sugarcandy Mountain were lies, and yet they allowed him to remain on the farm, not working.

After his hind leg had healed up, Boxer worked harder than ever. All the animals worked like slaves that year. Apart from the regular work of the farm, and the rebuilding of the windmill, there was the schoolhouse for the young pigs, which was started in March. Sometimes the long hours with less food were hard to bear. But Boxer never lost his heart. However, his power was not what it had been. His appearance was a little changed.The others said, "Boxer will be better when the spring grass comes on." But the spring came and Boxer grew no better. Sometimes, when he worked hard on the hill, it seemed that nothing kept him on his feet except the wish to continue. At such times he usually said, "I will work harder." Once again Clover and Benjamin warned him to take care of his health, but Boxer paid no attention. His twelfth birthday was coming. He did not care about his birthday. All he wanted was to build the windmill before he went on pension.

One day in the summer, a sudden rumour ran round the farm that something had happened to Boxer. He went out alone to drag a load of stone down to the windmill. And the rumour was true. A few minutes later two pigeons came flying in with the news:

"Boxer has fallen! He is lying on the ground and can't get up!"

About half the animals on the farm ran out to the hill where the windmill stood. There lay Boxer on the ground. He could not even raise his head. A thin stream of blood had trickled out of his mouth. Clover dropped to her knees at his side.

"Boxer!" she cried, "how are you?"

"It is my lung," said Boxer. "It does not matter. I think you will finish the windmill without me. I have collected a pretty good store of stones. I had only another month to live in any case. To tell you the truth, I waited for my retirement. And, perhaps, as Benjamin is growing old too, they will let him retire at the same time and be a companion to me."

"We must get help at once," said Clover. "Run, somebody, and tell Squealer what has happened!"

All the other animals immediately ran back to the farmhouse to give Squealer the news. Only Clover remained, and Benjamin who lay down at Boxer's side, and, without speaking. He kept the flies off him with his long tail. After about a quarter of an hour Squealer came. He looked confused. He said that Comrade Napoleon had learned about this misfortune. He was already making arrangements to send Boxer to the hospital at Willingdon. The animals felt a little scared at this. Except for Mollie and Snowball, no other animal had ever left the farm. They did not like to think of their sick comrade in the hands of human beings. However, Squealer easily convinced them that the veterinary surgeon in Willingdon could treat Boxer better than anyone could do on the farm. And about half an hour later, when Boxer somewhat recovered, got onto his feet with difficulty, he went back to his stall slowly. There Clover and Benjamin prepared a good bed of straw for him. For the next two days Boxer remained in his stall. The pigs sent out a large bottle of pink medicine which they had found in the medicine chest in the bathroom. Clover gave it to Boxer twice a day after meals. In the evenings she lay in his stall and talked to him, while Benjamin kept the flies off him. Boxer tried not to be sorry for what had happened. If he made a good recovery, he would live another three years. He looked forward to the peaceful days that he would spend in the corner of the big pasture. It would be the first time that he had time to think of his retirement. He wished, he said, to devote the rest of his life to learning the remaining twenty-two letters of the alphabet.

Benjamin and Clover could only be with Boxer after working hours. It was in the middle of the day when the van came to take him away. The animals were all at work working in the field under the supervision of a pig. They were surprised to see Benjamin come running from the direction of the farm buildings, crying at the top of his voice. It was the first time that they had ever seen Benjamin excited.

"Quickly, quickly!" he shouted. "Come at once! They are taking Boxer away!"

Without waiting for orders from the pig, the animals left their work and ran back to the farm buildings. They saw in the yard a large closed van. A fat man was sitting on the driver's seat. And Boxer's stall was empty. The animals crowded around the van.

"Good-bye, Boxer!" they said. "Good-bye!"

"Fools! Fools!" shouted Benjamin. "Fools! Do you not see what is written on the side of that van?"

The animals tried to read the inscription on the van. Muriel began to spell out the words. But Benjamin stepped forward and read aloud:

"Alfred Simmonds, Horse Slaughterer, Willingdon. Do you not understand what that means? They are taking Boxer to his death!"

All the animals cried with horror. At this moment the van moved out of the yard quickly. All the animals followed, crying out at the tops of their voices. Clover tried to run as quickly as she could. The van began to gather speed.

"Boxer!" she cried. "Boxer! Boxer! Boxer!"

And just at this moment, she saw Boxer's face, with the white stripe down his nose, at the small window at the back of the van.

"Boxer!" cried Clover in a terrible voice. "Boxer! Get out! Get out quickly! They are taking you to your death!"

All the animals began to cry:

"Get out, Boxer, get out!"

But the van was already gathering speed and drawing away from them. It was unclear whether Boxer had understood what Clover had said. But a moment later his face disappeared from the window and there was the sound of the drumming of hoofs inside the van. He was trying to kick his way out. Unfortunately, his power had left him. In a few moments, the sound of drumming hoofs stopped. In desperation, the animals began to cry bitterly. Boxer's face did not reappear at the window. It was too late.The van quickly disappeared down the road. They never saw Boxer again. Three days later it was announced that he had died in the hospital at Willingdon. He had received every attention a horse could have. Squealer came to announce the news to the others. He said that he had been present during Boxer's last hours.

"It was the most terrible thing I have ever seen!" said Squealer, lifting his trotter and wiping away a tear. "I was at his bedside at the very last. And at the end, almost too weak to speak, he said to me that his single sorrow was to die before the windmill was finished. "Forward, comrades!" he said. "Forward in the name of the Rebellion. Long live Animal Farm! Long live Comrade Napoleon! Napoleon is always right." Those were his very last words, comrades."

Here Squealer's face suddenly changed. He fell silent for a moment, and his little eyes moved suspiciously from side to side before he continued.

"I heard some stupid rumours," he continued. "Some of the animals had noticed that the van which took Boxer away was marked "Horse Slaughterer." Some animals think that Boxer had been sent to his death. It is almost unbelievable that any animal could be so stupid.Comrades, the explanation is very simple. The van had previously belonged to the horse slaughterer. A veterinary surgeon had bought it a few weeks ago. He had not yet painted the old name out. That was how the mistake had arisen."

The animals were glad to hear this. And when Squealer went on to give further details of Boxer's death – bed, the admirable care, the expensive medicines – their last doubts disappeared and they were happy to know that at least he had died happy. Napoleon himself came to the meeting on the following Sunday morning and pronounced a short speech in Boxer's honour. It had not been possible, he said, to bring back their comrade's body to Animal Farm.But he had ordered a large wreath to be made from the flowers in the farmhouse garden.

He sent this wreath to be placed on Boxer's grave.Napoleon ended his speech with Boxer's two favourite phrases, "I will work harder" and "Comrade Napoleon is always right." These were phrases, he said, which every animal should follow.

One day later, a grocer's van drove up from Willingdon and delivered a large wooden box at the farmhouse. That night there was the sound of loud singing, which was followed by a violent quarrel and ended at about eleven o'clock with a crash of glass. No one moved in the farmhouse before noon on the following day, and the word went round that from somewhere or other the pigs had gotten the money to buy themselves another case of whisky.

## Chapter 10

Years passed. The seasons came and went, and the short animal lives fled by. A time came when no one remembered the old days before the Rebellion, except Clover, Benjamin, Moses, and a number of the pigs. Muriel was dead. Bluebell, Jessie, and Pincher were dead. Jones too was dead. He had died in another part of the country. Snowball was forgotten. Boxer was forgotten, except by the few who had known him. Clover was an old mare now. She was two years past the retiring age, but, in fact, no animal had ever actually retired. The talk of setting aside a pasture for retired animals had been forgotten long ago. Napoleon was now a huge boar. Squealer was so fat that he could with difficulty see out of his eyes. Only old Benjamin was much the same as ever. He was a little greyer about the muzzle. Since Boxer's death, he was more silent than ever. There were many more animals on the farm now, though the increase was not so great as had been expected in earlier years. Many animals had been born to whom the Rebellion was only a dim tradition, passed on by word of mouth. Napoleon had bought three horses who had never heard about the Rebellion before their arrival. The farm had three horses now besides Clover. They were strong horses, good workers and comrades, but very stupid. None of them could learn the alphabet beyond the letter B. They accepted everything about the Rebellion and the principles of Animalism. But it was doubtful whether they understood very much of it.

The farm was more prosperous now. It was better organized. Napoleon enlarged it by two fields which he had bought from

Mr Pilkington. The windmill had been successfully finished at last. The farm had a threshing machine and a hay elevator, and various new buildings. The windmill was not used for generating electrical power. It was used for milling corn and brought in a good profit. The animals worked hard to build another windmill. The animals never talked about the luxuries of which Snowball had once talked in the past – the stalls with electric light, hot and cold water, and the three-day week. Napoleon told them that such ideas were contrary to the spirit of Animalism. The truest happiness, he said, lay in working hard and living simply. Somehow it seemed that the farm had grown richer without making the animals themselves any richer, except, of course, for the pigs and the dogs. Perhaps this was because there were so many pigs and so many dogs. It was not that these creatures did not work, after their fashion. Squealer was never tired of explaining the endless work in the supervision and organization of the farm. Much of this work was of a kind that other animals were too stupid to understand. For example, Squealer told them that the pigs had to spend every day on mysterious things called "files," "reports," "minutes," and "memoranda." These were large sheets of paper which were covered with writing. These sheets were very important for the welfare of the farm, Squealer said. But still, the pigs and dogs never produced any food by their work. Besides, there were very many of them, and their appetites were always good.

As for the others, their life, so far as they knew, was as it had always been. They were generally hungry, they slept on straw, they drank from the pool, they worked hard in the field. In winter they were troubled by the cold, and in summer by the flies. Sometimes the older ones among them tried to determine whether, in the early days of the Rebellion, things had been better or worse than now. They could not remember. There was nothing with which they could compare their present lives. They had nothing except Squealer's lists of figures, which invariably showed that everything was getting better and better. The animals could not solve this problem. Anyway, they had little time for thinking about such things now. Only old Benjamin could remember every detail of his long life. He knew that things never had been much better or much worse. Hunger, hard work, disappointment, and limited food were, he said, the unchangeable law of life. And yet the animals never gave up hope. More, they never lost, even for a moment, their sense of honour. They were members of Animal Farm. They were still the only farm in the whole county (in all England!) operated by animals. Not one of them, not even the youngest, not even the newcomers who had been brought from farms ten or twenty miles away, ever stopped to admire that. And when they heard the gun booming and saw the green flag fluttering, their hearts were full of pride, and the talk turned always towards the old heroic days, the escape of Jones, the writing of the Seven Commandments, the great battles in which the human beings had been defeated. The animals had not forgotten their old dreams. They still believed in the Republic of the Animals, with the green fields of England without human beings. Someday it would come. It might not be soon. But still it would come. They even sang the song of *the Beasts of England* secretly here and there. It was a fact that every animal on the farm knew it, though no one dared to sing it aloud. Their lives were hard and not all of their hopes had been fulfilled, but they knew that they were not as other animals. If they went hungry, it was not because of cruel human beings. If they worked hard, at least they worked for themselves. No creature among them went on two legs. No creature called any other creature "Master." All animals were equal.

One day in early summer, Squealer ordered the sheep to follow him. He led them out to a piece of waste ground at the other end of the farm. The sheep spent the whole day there browsing at the leaves under Squealer's supervision. In the evening he returned to the farmhouse himself. He told the sheep to stay where they were. They remained there for a whole week. During that time the other animals did not see them. Squealer was with them for the greater part of every day. He was, he said, teaching them to sing a new song. One week ago, the sheep returned to the barn. The animals finished work and were making their way back to the farm buildings. Suddenly, they heard a terrible cry of a horse sounded from the yard. The animals were scared. It was Clover's voice. She cried again, and all the animals ran quickly into the yard. Then they saw what Clover had seen. It was a pig walking on his hind legs! Yes, it was Squealer. He walked slowly, but with perfect balance. And a moment later, out from the door of the farmhouse came a long line of pigs. They were all walking on their hind legs. Some did it better than others, but every one of them made his way right round the yard successfully. And, finally, there was a loud barking of dogs and Napoleon came out himself. He was walking on his hind legs perfectly. He was looking from side to side. His dogs were walking around him. He carried a whip in his trotter.

There was a deadly silence. The animals were scared and terrified.They watched the long line of pigs walk slowly around the yard. It was as though the world had turned upside-down. Then there came a moment when the first shock seemed to pass, but even now they were too scared to say some word of protest. But just at that moment, as though at a signal, all the sheep began to sing the following song:

*"Four legs good, two legs BETTER! Four legs good, two legs BETTER! Four legs good, two legs BETTER!"*

The sheep were singing the song for five minutes without stopping. And by the time the sheep stopped singing, the chance to say any protest passed. The pigs walked back into the farmhouse. Benjamin looked at Clover. Her old eyes looked dimmer than ever. Without saying anything, she went to the barn, where the Seven Commandments were written. Benjamin followed her. For a minute or two, they stood looking at the wall with its black letters.

"I do not see well," she said finally. "But it seems to me that that wall looks different. Are the Seven Commandments the same, Benjamin?"

Benjamin read out to her what was written on the wall. There was nothing there now except a single Commandment. It ran:

ALL ANIMALS ARE EQUAL
BUT SOME ANIMALS ARE MORE EQUAL
THAN OTHERS

After that, it did not seem strange when the next day the pigs who were supervising the work of the farm all carried whips in their trotters. It did not seem strange to learn that the pigs had bought a telephone and installed it in the farmhouse. It did not seem strange when Napoleon walked in the farmhouse garden with a pipe in his mouth. It did not even seem strange when the pigs took Mr Jones's clothes out of the wardrobes and put them on. Napoleon himself wore a black coat and leather leggings, while his sow wore a silk dress which Mrs Jones had been wearing on Sundays. A week later, in the afternoon, five farmers came to the farm. Napoleon invited them to make a tour of inspection. They walked all over the farm and expressed great admiration for everything they saw, especially the windmill. The animals were working on the field. They worked hard raising their faces from the ground now and then. They were frightened both of the pigs and the human visitors. That evening loud laughter and singing came from the farmhouse. And suddenly, at the sound of the mixed voices, the animals were very curious. What could be happening in there? They began to creep as quietly as possible into the farmhouse garden. At the gate, they stopped because they were frightened to go on. Clover led the way in. They walked silently up to the house, and the tall animals as they were tall, looked in at the dining-room window. There, round the long table, sat five farmers and five large pigs. Napoleon occupied the seat of honour at the head of the table. The pigs seemed very comfortable in their chairs. The company were enjoying a game of cards. They stopped playing for a moment to drink a toast. A large jug was circulating, and the glasses were refilled with beer. No one noticed the wondering faces of the animals that looked in at the window. Mr Pilkington, the owner of Foxwood, stood up, with his glass in his hand. In a moment, he said, he would ask the company to drink a toast. But before doing so, there were a few words that he wanted to say.

"I am glad that a long period of misunderstanding has come to an end," said Mr Pilkington. "There were many unlucky accidents and mistaken ideas. We, farmers, had been afraid of the farm owned and operated by pigs. It seemed so unusual to us! Too many farmers had thought that on such farm indiscipline would prevail someday.We had been nervous about its effects on our animals, or even on our human employees. But all such doubts are now dispelled. Today we visited Animal Farm and inspected every part of it with our own eyes. And what did we find? Not only the most up-to-date methods, but also discipline and order which should be an example for farmers everywhere. The lower animals on Animal Farm do more work and receive less food than the pigs in the country. To tell the truth, today I saw many methods which I want to introduce on my farm immediately. I think other farmers at this table agree with me on this matter."

He stopped for a moment. Then he continued:

"There should be friendship between Animal Farm and its neighbours. There was no friendship between pigs and human beings before. But there should be friendship between us now! I hope that there will be a long friendship between Animal Farm and its neighbours. There should not be any clash of interests between pigs and human beings. From now on, we will have neither difficulties nor struggles. I believe that all animals are not equal. There must be a strict division between higher and lower classes of animals. Dear pigs, I congratulate you on the low rations, long working hours, and the general absence of luxury among the lower class of animals! And now, dear gentlemen, I ask you to rise to your feet and make sure that your glasses are full. Now, gentlemen, I give you a toast: To the prosperity of Animal Farm!"

There was an enthusiastic roar at the table. Napoleon was so glad that he left his place and came round the table to clink his glass against Mr Pilkington's before emptying it. When the roar stopped, Napoleon, who remained on his feet, said to the company that he too had a few words to say.

Like all of Napoleon's speeches, it was short and to the point.

"I am happy that the period of misunderstanding has come to an end now," said Napoleon. "There had been rumours that we had been trying to cause a rebellion among the animals of the neighbouring farms. That was a lie, of course! Our single wish, now and in the past, was to live at peace and in normal business relations with our neighbours. Animal Farm which I have the honour to control, is a co-operative enterprise. I have made certain changes in the routine of the farm. For example, the pigs address each other as "Comrade." The lower animals have no right to do so. You, Mr Pilkington, called our farm "Animal Farm" in your speech. You do not know that the name "Animal Farm" has been changed. It is known as "Manor Farm" now. It is its correct and original name. Gentlemen, I will give you the same toast as before, but in a different form. Fill your glasses with a beer! Gentlemen, here is my toast: To the prosperity of Manor Farm!"

There was the same loud cry as before. But as the animals outside looked at the scene, it seemed to them that some strange thing was happening. Something had changed in the faces of the pigs. Clover looked from one face to another. Some of them had five chins, some of them four, some had three. But there was something strange on the pigs' faces. The applause at the table finally came to an end. The company took up their cards and continued their game. The animals crept silently away. A moment later they heard loud voices coming from the farmhouse. They ran back and looked through the window again. There was a loud quarrel. There were loud cries, suspicious glances, and angry denials at the table. The thing was that Napoleon and Mr Pilkington had tricked each other in the game simultaneously. Ten voices were screaming in anger. Now it was obvious what had happened to the faces of the pigs. The animals outside looked from pigs to men, and from men to pigs again. But already it was impossible to say which was which.

**THE END**

# *Glossary*

**absorbed** – emmek
**abundance** – bolluk, bereket
**achievement** – kazanım, başarı
**act** – davranmak, hareket etmek
**admire** – hayran kalmak
**admit** – kabul etmek
**anniversary** – yıl dönümü kutlaması
**apathy** – ilgisizlik
**appearance** – görünüş
**appetite** – iştah
**argue** – tartışmak
**articulate** – konuşkan
**attentively** – dikkatlice
**badge** – rozet
**bare** – çıplak
**barley** – arpa
**barn** – ahır
**beak** – gaga
**beam** – kiriş
**bear** – katlanmak
**beast** – hayvan
**benefit** – fayda, yarar
**blacksmithing** – demircilik
**boar** – erkek domuz
**bothering** – zahmet
**brass** – prinç
**breeding** – yetiştirme
**brewing** – mayalama
**brood** – kuluçkadan çıkan yavrular
**bullet** – mermi
**bursting** – patlamak
**bushel** – ölçek
**carpentering** – marangozluk
**cart** – at arabası
**cement** – çimento
**chase** – kovalamak, takip etmek
**chew** – çiğnemek
**circulate** – yaymak, dolaşmak
**climate** – iklim
**clover** – yonca
**collar** – tasma
**commandments** – emirler
**companion** – arkadaş
**complained** – şikayet etmek
**comrade** – yoldaş
**conquer** – yenmek
**conquered** – ele geçirmek
**consumes** – tüketir
**contentedly** – memnuniyetle
**convince** – ikna etmek
**creature** – yaratık, varlık
**creep** – sokulmak, sürünmek
**crowbar** – levye
**cruel** – zalim, merhametsiz
**crust** – kabuk, tortu
**cud** – geviş
**cunning** – marifetli; kurnaz
**curious** – meraklı
**dare** – cesaret etmek
**debate** – tartışma, müzakere
**decision** – karar
**dew** – çiy, damlacık
**dim** – bulanık
**dimmer** – daha donuk
**disappeared** – ortadan kaybolmak
**discussion** – tartışma

**dispute** – tartışma, münakaşa
**distilling** – damıtma
**divided** – ayrılmış, bölünmüş
**doom** – kıyamet
**doubtful** – şüpheli, kuşkulu
**drifted** – yığılmak
**drop** – damla
**duty** – görev, yükümlülük
**effort** – çaba
**enemy** – düşman
**engage in trade** – ticaret yapmak
**enthusiastic** – hevesli, coşkulu
**equal** – eşit
**escape** – kaçma, kurtulma
**evil** – kötülük
**except** – hariç
**excitement** – heyecan, coşku
**existence** – varoluş
**expelled** – kovulmuş
**explanation** – açıklama
**exploit** – istismar, sömürmek
**expressed** – ifade
**faithful** – sadık, bağlı, vefalı
**fang** – azı dişi
**fate** – kader; son
**feather** – kuş tüyü
**fertile** – bereketli
**field** – tarla, kır
**flutter** – heyecan, telaş
**foal** – tay
**forelock** – perçem, kakül
**frank** – dürüst, açık sözlü, samimi
**gathering** – toplama
**grane** – tahıl, tane
**growl** – hırlamak, hırıltı
**gun** – silah
**habit** – huy, alışkanlık
**hammer** – çekiç
**harness** – koşum takımı
**harrow** – tırmık
**harvest** – hasat
**hay** – saman
**hedge** – çit
**hesitate** – tereddüt etmek
**hind** – arka
**hoisting** – çekmek, kaldırmak
**hoof (hooves)** – toynak
**hope** –umut
**horn** – boynuz
**inevitable** – kaçınılmaz
**influence** – etki, tesir
**inn** – meyhane
**instant** – anında
**inventive** – yaratıcı
**irrepressible** – önlenemez, durdurulamaz
**jealous** – kıskanç
**kind** – tür, çeşit
**laborious** – zahmetli, yorucu
**lantern** – fener
**lash** – kamçı darbesi; kamçılamak
**launch** – başlatmak
**lawsuit** – dava
**leisure** – boş zaman, rahat
**liberty** – özgürlük
**loyalty** – sadakat, bağlılık
**lump** – parça
**majority** – çoğunluk

**mane** – yele
**mantelpiece** – şömine rafı
**mare** – kısrak
**marvel** – hayret etmek
**mash** – lapa, püre
**mattress** – şilte, yatak
**miserable** – sefil, perişan, zavallı
**misery** – acı, sefalet
**mistaken** – yanlış hatalı
**motto** – slogan, parola
**muted** – sağır etmek
**mysterious** – gizemli, esrarengiz
**neglected** – bakımsız
**nestled** – sokulmak
**nodded** – başı ile onaylamak
**oat** – yulaf
**occupied** - meşgul
**opponents** – rakipler
**orchard** – meyve bahçesi
**order** – emir
**pail** – kova
**pasture** – otlak, çayır
**paw** – pati, pençe
**pecking** – gagalamak
**perch** - tünemek, konmak
**persuade** – ikna etmek
**phrase** – ifade
**pile of timber** – kereste yığını
**pipe** – pipo
**plough** – pulluk
**ploughland** – sürülebilir toprak
**poem** – şiir
**poison** – zehir
**pond** – gölet
**porker** – domuz
**precautions** – önlemler
**predict** – önceden haber vermek
**preparation** – hazırlık
**prevail** – galip gelmek, yenmek
**previous** – önceki, evvelki
**primitive** – ilkel
**principle** – prensip, ilke
**produce** – üretmek, yetiştirmek
**prophecy** – kehanet
**prosperity** – refah, zenginlik
**prosperous** – refah, zengin
**proud** – guru duymak
**purpose** – amaç
**purred** – hırıldamak, mırıldamak
**pursuing** – peşinde
**rafter** – çatı kirişi
**raise** – kaldırmak, yükseltmek
**ration** – yiyecek payı
**raven** – karga
**rebellion** – isyan, ayaklanma
**rebuild** – yeniden inşa etmek
**reduced** – indirgenmiş
**regarded** – saygın
**reign** – egemenlik, hükümdarlık
**rein** – dizgin
**remark** – açıklama
**remove** – uzaklaştırmak
**resemble** – benzemek
**resolution** – kararlılık
**retreat** – geri çekilmek
**ribben** – kurdele
**ridiculous** – saçma, anlamsız
**ripe** – olgun

**rubbish heap** – çöplük
**ruin** – harabe
**rumour** – söylenti, dedikodu
**sacrifice** – fedakarlık
**sake** – hatır
**sand** – kum
**scattered** – dağıtmak
**scent** – koku, esans
**schedule** – programlamak, çalışma saatlerini yazmak
**scheme** – şema, plan
**seldom** – nadiren
**sentimental** – duygusal
**settled** – oturmuş
**shed** – kulübe
**sill** – eşik, pervaz
**situated** – kurulu, bulunan
**slave** – esir, köle
**sniff** – koklamak
**soil** – toprak
**soul** – ruh
**sow** – ekmek, tohum ekmek
**spread** – yayılmış
**stable** – ahır
**stalk** – sap
**stall** – ahır
**staring** – dik dik bakmak
**starve** – açlıktan ömek
**steadily** – sürekli
**stir** – ayağa kaldırmak
**store** – ambar
**straw** – saman
**stray** – başıboş
**strip** – şerit
**stroke** – okşamak
**struggle** – savaş, mücadele
**suffer** – acı çekmek; katlanmak
**sweated** – terli
**tame** – evcil
**task** – görev, iş
**tears** – gözyaşı
**threshing** – harman
**tool** – alet
**tormentor** – işkenceci
**trace** – iz, işaret
**treachery** – ihanet
**trembled** – titremek
**tremendous** – muazzam
**triumph** – zafer
**trotter** – tırıs giden at; paça
**tyranny** – zulüm, zorbalık
**udder** – meme
**vain** – nafile, boşuna
**voluntary** - gönüllü
**vote** – oy
**wagged** – sallamak
**weed** – yabani ot
**well** – kuyu
**wheat** – buğday
**whip** – kırbaç
**whirling** – fıldır fıldır dönmek
**windmill** – yel değirmeni
**wing** – kanat
**wisdom** – bilgelik
**wise** – bilge, akıllı
**wisp** – tutam, ufacık şey
**worth** – değerli
**yard** – avlu

# *Activities*

## A) TRUE OR FALSE

1) Old Major was an old horse with a white strip on his nose. **T F**

2) Old Major saw a dream in which there were no human beings on earth. **T F**

3) The Rebellion happened much earlier than the animals had expected. **T F**

4) Many animals were killed in the Battle of the Cowshed. **T F**

5) There were Nine Commandments written on the wall of the barn. **T F**

6) The pigs were the main brainworkers on Animal Farm. **T F**

7) Snowball was expelled from the farm for stealing food. **T F**

8) The animals built the windmill successfully at the first attempt. **T F**

9) The animals never spoke out against Napoleon's new rules in the organization of the farm. **T F**

10) The pigs lived in the farmhouse and imitated human beings' behaviour and habits whenever possible. **T F**

## B) CHOOSE THE CORRECT ANSWER

1. Who predicted the Rebellion on the farm?

   A) Old Major
   B) Snowball
   C) Napoleon
   D) Benjamin

2. What did Snowball paint on the flag of Animal Farm?

   A) a tree B) a hoof and a horn
   C) a bird D) a pig

3. How many commandments were written on the wall of the barn?

   A) 7 B) 9
   C) 10 D) 8

4. In what way did Napoleon expel Snowball from the farm?

   A) He accused him of stealing food.
   B) He won a leadership fight.
   C) He ordered his huge dogs to attack Snowball.
   D) He accused Snowball of being Jones'agent.

5. How did the animals' lives change after Snowball's exile?

   A) They worked less and ate more food.
   B) They worked like slaves and were hungry all the time.
   C) They became lazy and refused to work on the fields.
   D) They worked three days a week.

6. "I will work harder." Who mentioned this phrase very often?

   A) Benjamin
   B) Clover
   C) Squealer
   D) Boxer

7. What did Moses often mention in his talks?

   A) Sugarcandy Mountain
   B) His life during Jones' reign
   C) Other farms in the country
   D) The news from Willingdon

8. Who followed Napoleon whenever he left the farmhouse?

   A) Squealer
   B) A cat
   C) His huge dogs
   D) All the other pigs

9. Why did Napoleon begin to trade with human beings?

   A) He wanted to earn money for himself.
   B) He wanted to build a new barn for the animals.
   C) He wanted to trick human beings.
   D) He wanted to prove that animals could trade quite as well as human beings.

10. With whom did Napoleon play cards at the end of the novel?

   A) with Mr Whymper
   B) with Mr Jones
   C) with Snowball
   D) with Mr Pilkington and the other farmers of neighbouring farms

## C) ANSWER THE QUESTIONS

1. Which animal sang Beast of England for the first time? What was this song about?

   ..........................................................................................

2. What caused the Rebellion on the farm?

   ..........................................................................................

3. How did the animals' lives change after the Rebellion?

   ..........................................................................................

4. Who wrote the Seven Commandments on the wall? What were they about?

   ..........................................................................................

5. Why did Mollie leave the farm? Did she do it willingly?

   ..........................................................................................

6. What did Napoleon and Snowball always argue about? Whom do you support in those arguments?

   ..........................................................................................

7. Did Snowball ever come back to Animal Farm after his exile?

   ..........................................................................................

8. Who was Napoleon's own bodyguard? Did Napoleon ever walk alone?

   ..........................................................................................

9. What kind of new rules did Napoleon impose as a leader of Animal Farm?

   ..........................................................................................

10. Did Napoleon's new rules violate the Seven Commandments?

   ..........................................................................................

11. Who was Squealer? Describe his character.

..........................................................................................

12. How did the animals build the windmill? Did Napoleon and the other pigs help them in that hard work?

..........................................................................................

13. How was the first windmill destroyed?

..........................................................................................

14. Why did Napoleon and the other pigs move to the farmhouse? How did they explain the reasons for that?

..........................................................................................

15. Did the pigs work and eat as much as the other animals on the farm?

..........................................................................................

16. What kind of celebrations did the animals have on Animal Farm?

..........................................................................................

17. Why did Napoleon order the animals to sow the barley? In what way did he plan to use it?

..........................................................................................

18. Why did Napoleon begin to trade with human beings?

..........................................................................................

19. Who took Boxer away from Animal Farm in the van? Did Boxer ever come back to Animal Farm?

..........................................................................................

20. How did the novel end?

..........................................................................................